"You're blind and you're prejudiced."

Once started, Lucy went on. "Do you honestly think the Italian aristocracy would be better if they kept intermarrying?"

"It would protect them from grasping women who think they've hit the jackpot," he said grimly.

"You know nothing about my sister! I hope all Italian men aren't as intransigent as you," she said scathingly. She stood with dignity. "You'd better put the cost of the meal on my bill. I'd hate you to think *I* was a grasping woman."

Max leaned back in his chair, his eyes calculating, his face stony. "Tell her it was a good try."

Lucy's brow furrowed, not understanding. "Where's Massimo Mazzardi? I want to speak to him."

"Damn you!" roared Max. "Drop the innocence. You know perfectly well that *I'm* Mazzardi!"

SARA WOOD lives in a rambling sixteenth-century home in the medieval town of Lewes amid the Sussex hills. Her sons have claimed the cellar for bikes, making ferret cages, taxidermy and winemaking, while Sara has virtually taken over the study with her reference books, word processor and what have you. Her amiable, tolerant husband, she says, squeezes in wherever he finds room. After having tried many careers—secretary, guest house proprietor, play-group owner and primary teacher—she now finds writing romance novels gives her enormous pleasure.

Books by Sara Wood

Don't miss any of our special offers. Write to us at the following address for information on our newest releases.

Harlequin Reader Service
901 Fuhrmann Blvd., P.O. Box 1397, Buffalo, NY 14240
Canadian address: P.O. Box 603,
Fort Erie, Ont. L2A 5X3

SARA WOOD

love not dishonour

Harlequin Books

TORONTO • NEW YORK • LONDON
AMSTERDAM • PARIS • SYDNEY • HAMBURG
STOCKHOLM • ATHENS • TOKYO • MILAN

Harlequin Presents first edition November 1990
ISBN 0-373-11318-8

Original hardcover edition published in 1989
by Mills & Boon Limited

CHAPTER ONE

LUCINDA was about to check her list of duties on the back of the kitchen door when her eyes fell on her sister's most recent letter. Her small, slender hand reached out and searched for one particular comment, written in Selina's usual brief, scrawling style.

'...absolutely heavenly place, the owner must be as rich as Croesus. I'm hoping against hope that I'll bump into him one moonlit night under the hibiscus. So romantic! Don't laugh. You miss a lot, you sensible old thing!'

Sensible. Lucy smiled quietly and pushed the letter back under the toaster. The early September sun flooded the kitchen with gentle gold, burnishing her carrot-coloured hair till she possessed a glowing halo. Yes, she was practical, realistic and renowned for her preference for plain living. But...once in a while she yearned for something magical to happen.

In the meantime, there was the ironing! Lucy studied the duty list first, as a matter of habit. Coffee and biscuits had been served, the meat delivery checked and stored, the laundry boxed, and Mrs Knight had been turned in bed. Not on the list was Mrs Baker's tangled knitting or the spilt jug of water or getting Mrs Knight's budgie back into its cage, but Lucy had fitted them in too, with her usual calm capability. Everything was going smoothly, as usual.

Satisfied, she retied the navy ribbon which confined her thick hair at the nape of her neck. All the elderly

people at Park View Rest Home loved her hair—the only
gaudy splash of colour about her—but that was because
of its old-fashioned style: drawn back from her small,
fine-boned face to be caught at the nape of her neck and
then flowing freely in a mass of untameable Renaissance
waves, right down to her waist.

Twenty-three years' worth of waves! She grinned, set
up the ironing board and selected a blouse from the
overflowing basket. By the time she reached eighty, she'd
need a couple of carrier bags to contain her hair and
stop it trailing on the ground! It was a 'no maintenance'
style, a 'dry while you work' one—and that was essential here. Selina's dreams were all very well, but not
much help in running the Home. Still, she had to admit
that over the last three weeks, since Selina had decided
to look for adventure and employment on the continent,
life had been quieter and less of a strain.

No more lovelorn young men, no more chaos in the
bedroom the two girls shared and no dramas. Awfully
dull! Lucy ran the iron over the crisp cotton. They all
missed bubbly Selina, especially Lionel, who
worshipped her.

'Lucy!' called her stepfather from the lounge. 'Help!
I'm being swallowed alive!'

'Serves you right, Lionel,' she answered, her hazel eyes
dancing with amusement. He was carrying out his threat
to criticise a much-loved soap opera. With nine elderly
ladies against him—one of them Lucy's mother—he
hadn't a chance!

She was tempted by the laughter, though. Blow the
ironing! It could be tackled during her lunch break. That
would stop her from re-reading Selina's letter about palm
trees and exotic flowers and fairy-tale *palazzos*, and
feeling a tug of restless energy as a result!

However, Lionel was denied her spirited defence because the telephone rang, just as her slender body, disguised by a baggy but practical nylon overall, was squeezing past the ironing board.

'Reinforcements delayed, Dad!' she called, giggling at his theatrical groan. She shut the lounge door to block out the jollity. 'Park View Rest Home, can I help you?' she asked in her firm voice.

'Lucy! Thank heaven it's you! I'm in trouble. I need you.'

Oh, no, she thought. Not again! Poor Selina.

'Calm down,' she said to her half-sister. 'Stop screeching in my ear, love. Where are you?'

'Italy still, Lake Maggiore. Didn't you get my last letter?' asked Selina impatiently.

'Yes. You said everything was wonderful and you...'

'Well, it's not *now*! Listen, I haven't much time because I've sneaked away from work. I need cash, Lucy, lots of it.'

'Oh.' Lucy gave a small, disappointed sigh. The harum-scarum Selina was always short of money. 'Won't your boss lend you some against next week's wages?'

'Huh! Massimo Mazzardi won't even lend a helping hand to his aged grandmother, let alone his lowly staff,' said Selina with a choke in her voice. 'Besides, he's the one I owe money to. I'll repay whatever you bring, but I must have it now.'

'Bring? I can't leave everyone here and...'

'You must! It won't reach me quickly enough otherwise. Money transfers can take days. You have to come.'

Selina began to sob, and Lucy's white brow furrowed in worry. This didn't sound like an ordinary disaster. Because she was reckless and took risks with her life, Selina frequently found herself in trouble. Add blonde fluffy curls, an innocent sex appeal and an hour-glass figure to that recklessness and it was no wonder that Lucy had long ago learnt how to deal with Selina's frustrated suitors and one or two creditors. But she'd never sounded so scared before. And even Selina was well aware that Lucy was indispensable as far as the Home was concerned. She must really be in a state to suggest that Lucy should abandon her charges and fly out to Italy.

'You're not thinking straight, Selina! Even if I could come, I haven't any cash, not enough to get me to Italy and back and to pay off this man. This isn't some kind of blackmail or protection racket, is it?' she asked.

'Sort of.' Selina's voice rose hysterically. 'You do have cash, in the building society. Bring that; all of it. Believe me, I wouldn't ask unless it was vital. I have to repay Mazzardi immediately. I can't stay in his debt—he's making the most sinister threats. I need *you*! Tell him I'm not a strumpet! I'm so frightened, Lucy, so terribly frightened!'

A strumpet? How short-sighted men were! Emotions were fighting within Lucy: sympathy, despair and anger. Her heart, always vulnerable to someone in trouble, had been given to Selina long ago when she first saw her soon after she was born. At three years old, Lucy already had a strong, caring streak within her and loved to look after her half-sister. Through school, she unobtrusively followed behind Selina, picking up the pieces of her life and smoothing everyone's ruffled feathers. Later, Lucy could see that no one realised Selina's difficulties as she lurched from one disastrous job to another without discovering her true potential. People only saw a beautiful girl, and that beauty blinded them to her inner qualities and brought desire from men and malicious envy from women.

Lucy's despair arose because the money mentioned by Selina had been put away towards a conservatory so that the residents could enjoy the spring and autumn sunshine without feeling chilled. Was it now to be thrown away on paying off some grasping employer? And, of course, she frowned, the creases deepening on her forehead, it would be a major undertaking to find someone to run the Home.

Her neat little mouth set in a hard, tight line. Mazzardi sounded an unpleasant bit of work if he was demanding sex in return for the money she'd borrowed.

'Don't worry about a thing, Selina. Leave it all to me. I'll sort everything out. I need this Mazzardi's address so I can write a letter to this man tonight. He'll think twice about bothering you after that, I guarantee,' she said briskly.

'No!' Selina wailed. 'You've got to come! Don't let me down. He's inhuman! He means every threat he makes! Lucy, I must go now, someone's coming. Get out here by tomorrow evening. Hotel Borromeo, Pescatori. Save me from this man!'

The last words had been gabbled and the connection broken. Either Selina had put the receiver down abruptly or someone had cut her off.

Lucy looked down and saw that her hands were trembling. Somehow Selina had angered a vicious-minded Italian who wouldn't take no for an answer. Visions of cinema gangsters flashed before her eyes, till common sense took over and she forced herself to think more rationally.

It sounded as though Selina needed a strong shoulder, a loving cuddle and then some sisterly advice about damping down her allure! And, not unusually, she needed some spirited defence.

Lucy considered all angles, with her usual thoroughness. A flying visit *was* possible, she supposed, providing she could arrange a stand-in—and that depended on the right person being available. She couldn't possibly leave the Home in the hands of anyone. Caring for the elderly was far more complicated a matter than just attending to their physical needs. On the few occasions when Lucy had not been there, the residents were always relieved to see her back again. They were her family and she was protective of them all.

But so was Selina, and she was in greater need. She'd go. Outwardly Lucy appeared unflustered as she made a few quick telephone calls. Inside, knowing that she'd have to move fast, she felt as though every part of her had been set on overdrive. Her mind buzzed with the thousand and one things she would need to do. Adrenalin had surged to give her the physical reserves she'd need to keep her tiny body going for the next forty-eight hours and to cope with the sick feeling in her stomach at Selina's plight. Already she hated Mazzardi for his callous behaviour. That man, she thought grimly, would regret ever meeting the two Parish sisters!

At last the social services came up with a temporary replacement, a pleasant lady who had taken over once before when Lucy had had flu. By skipping lunch, Lucy could get to the building society and see the travel agent about a flight. Then she'd have to pack and think up something to tell her mother and Lionel. Not the exact truth, of course, it would worry them too much.

Never before had she heard such abject fear in Selina's voice. The man was a monster! Lucy's hackles rose, thinking of the defenceless girl, alone and friendless in a foreign country, being intimidated by a pitiless, bullying employer.

Late that afternoon, Lucy took in the tea-trolley feeling unusually shaky. It wasn't in her nature to deceive anyone and the thought filled her with dismay.

'I have something to tell you all,' she said, when everyone had a cup of tea and the sandwiches were being passed around.

'Silence in court!' bellowed Lionel over the chatter, banging his spoon against the teapot.

Lucy winced at his choice of words. 'You know it's my birthday coming up in a couple of weeks——'

'I'm doing you a woolly scarf,' said Mrs Baker, waving something long, bright and full of holes at Lucy.

'Oh, what a lovely surprise!' She smiled, disconcerted. So that was what it was for! Everyone beamed back at her. That was the effect of one of Lucy's rare smiles, which transformed her small, serious face and turned her into a startling beauty. 'Well, Selina has asked me if I'll go to Italy for a couple of days——'

'Darling!' Her mother looked pleased. 'That's a wonderful idea! What a nice present for her to give you!'

'Er...yes.' Lucy looked at her feet, knowing that there was a telltale flush creeping up her porcelain face. 'The trouble is, it has to be tomorrow!'

There was silence in the room as they all digested this. Then Lionel laughed ruefully.

'Typical of Selina. Never gets things right. What are we going to do with her?' he asked everyone indulgently.

'Go,' said her mother firmly. 'Go and enjoy yourself. We'll manage. We've begged you to take a holiday for the last five years. What do you say?' she appealed to the friendly faces around her.

To Lucy's astonishment, they all agreed, seeming to take pleasure in Lucy's 'good fortune'. Emotion choked her as they began to bully her into packing straight away, and she ran from the room before she burst into mortified tears. They were all so sweet. It had been awful, not telling the whole truth. Nine ladies and one elderly man, all incapable of caring for themselves, dependent on her, urging her to dash off at a moment's notice and have a good time. She didn't deserve them. When she came back, she'd start baking secretly, so that they could celebrate her birthday in style!

It seemed that she was waving them all goodbye before she could catch her breath. The trip had been arranged in too much of a rush. Lucinda liked to plan carefully and work things out in meticulous detail. She wasn't mentally prepared, because she hadn't gone through every aspect of her trip to see every eventuality. Dreading her destination and what she might find, she withdrew into herself, preoccupied with her burdens.

The beauty of the alpine scenery, a thousand feet below the plane, passed by without Lucy noticing. Huge pillows of thick cloud rolled up the deep valleys, making a dense white barrier, broken only by the occasional thrusting, jagged mountain. Lucy had been worrying about everyone she'd left at home, then switching distractedly to thoughts of her sister, somewhere on an island in the middle of an Italian lake.

The flight from London to Milan seemed too quick. She wasn't ready for the stewardess's hand on her shoulder, jerking her from her inner world. Obediently she fastened her seat-belt, realising that the plane had already begun its descent and feeling sicker every minute from apprehension. Instinct told her that there was something sinister going on in Selina's life, and Lucy wondered whether she'd be able to cope. She was, after all, a small-town girl with no experience of the world outside. Ahead lay a confrontation with a faceless, fearsome foreigner who was powerful enough to terrify the bouncy, confident and totally optimistic Selina. How could an unsophisticated five-foot-two redhead cope? Lucy's stomach churned.

As she stepped out into the bright, dry heat, redolent with scented herbs drifting on the breeze, she bumped into a security guard. His hand clamped around her arm automatically in a vice-like grip and she realised how diminutive and insignificant she was beside him. He apologised politely, but Lucy had already registered his hard, masculine body and the pressure of the gun holster against her hip, and felt physically vulnerable. Her troubled eyes mutely followed his macho swagger as he walked away. She was a fool to think she could do battle with an influential and determined man, born in the same country that had raised Machiavelli!

It was too late to go home, however much she wanted to. Selina was depending on her to be strong. They'd outface the swine between them! Lucy's small body tensed in anticipation and her eyes hardened as she gripped her large shoulder-bag tightly. Engrossed in thought, she collected her case and queued for the minibus to Lake Maggiore.

Renzo Mazzardi waited in his brother's intimidatingly efficient-looking office, gulping down a large brandy. It was just like Massimo to keep him waiting—all part of his scheme to dominate people. The door-handle turned and Renzo's stomach muscles clenched in anticipation.

His brother's appearance made him shrink a little in the chair. There was a granite-like determination on

Massimo's face. The summons was bad news, then. Either Massimo was going to reprimand him for spending money again, or dredge up some minor mistake and magnify it out of all proportion.

Renzo took a comforting gulp of brandy. It was no good arguing with him, or trying to explain; he never listened. As a child, Massimo had been ferocious if anyone had crossed him—even adults. He had been fearless of punishment, scornful of their father's terrible biting words, and only the more resolute in his determination to stick to his beliefs.

Massimo quietly shut the massive panelled doors behind him, every move studied and deliberate. As always, apart from the pale gold shirt, he was dressed in black; a custom-made suit by Ferragamo's top designer. The conservative, timeless style contrasted with Renzo's more exotically patterned silk shirt and green pleat-waisted trousers. If there had been a contest between them, however, all eyes would have gravitated towards Massimo. Without moving a muscle—and there were plenty of those—he seemed to fill the room. He had an awesomely silent and unnerving presence, his fine features chiselled from unyielding stone, his dark eyes steady and remote.

There had been a magnetism about Massimo, even as a young man, but the years between had deepened that quality. Since he'd turned up a week ago, after twelve years' absence, Renzo had noticed that even in a roomful of extroverts Massimo's trick of silently standing apart would soon draw people to him.

'I've kept you waiting.'

Renzo gave a mirthless snort at his brother's statement, delivered in that strangely throaty voice. It had women falling over themselves in excitement. There was no apology, only the statement of fact: typical.

'I'm not a child, to be summoned to the headmaster's study,' he complained.

The dark, brooding eyes didn't even flicker. 'No. You are a man, with a man's responsibilities.'

That wasn't a very good start! Renzo could have kicked himself for walking into that one.

'I suppose you got involved in something even more important than me?' Renzo queried sarcastically.

'Some matters need immediate attention, some don't,' said Massimo, the normally gently persuasive manner holding more than a hint of sharpness. 'I hope you're not trying to suggest that I don't care about you. After all, I came when you asked me. I've abandoned my own business and left it to its own fate so that I can be here and help clear up father's estate.'

'We both inherited Isola Mazzardi,' bit Renzo. 'I don't see why I should do all the work and you take all the money.'

'No danger of that,' murmured Massimo. 'We seem to have made an equal division. *I* do all the work and *you* take all the money.'

'That's unfair!'

'Just like life. Your extravagances have created debt. Have I complained?'

'You've frozen my bank account and stopped all my credit. You rarely hit a man in the open—your style is to sneak behind him and pull away his chair!'

'How else can I control your debts? You bring us into dishonour. I can't have you tarnishing the Mazzardi name.' A small curl of disapproval had lifted Massimo's top lip.

'You did that long ago, when you ran away!' accused
Renzo. 'That broke Father's heart and the family
pride——'

He recoiled as Massimo was galvanised into action,
swallowing up the ground with his long strides. Renzo
had no time to rise and defend himself. Already, the big,
long-fingered hands were clamped on each arm of his
chair and his brother was leaning over him.

'Don't bring that up ever again,' he breathed. 'I came
here to discuss your relationship with that dizzy blonde,
not to rake up old wounds.'

'You *would* think that Selina is dizzy! She's intelli-
gent——'

'She can't tell the time,' growled Massimo.

'Lack of punctuality isn't a sign of low intel-
ligence——'

'It is when she knows that it makes me angry,' came
the sinister reply.

Renzo's eyes flared and he clutched his brother's
lapels. 'You hurt one hair of her head and I'll make you
sorry!' he yelled.

Massimo stared him down coldly till Renzo felt stupid
in the silence, gripping the jacket of a man who was so
much in control of his emotions that he had decided in
pure spite to cut his family out of his life.

'You're not worth fighting,' said Renzo in disgust. 'But
I'm going to tell you something that might shake your
self-control. I love Selina and I'm going to marry her!'

'Like hell you are.' Massimo looked scornful, but still
his voice was quiet and modulated. 'You'll make a decent
marriage to a woman who'll be a good mother and will
grace our name. We're not ordinary people, Renzo. We
are Mazzardis. We have a heritage to continue.'

'Snob! I will marry her. You'll see. Grandmamma likes her.'

'That's because she hasn't seen her as a future grand-daughter-in-law,' said Massimo drily. 'The girl is an obvious gold-digger and totally unreliable. She has no sense of duty whatsoever. This time, you'll not get your own way. All your life you've been spoilt. See what Selina thinks of you when she finds you have no money.'

'She won't care! We're in love. I won't let you interfere! I know my own mind.'

Massimo moved away and rested a negligent arm on the carved marble mantelpiece. 'Renzo, one of us has to be clear-headed. I care about your future happiness. I'm trying to save you from a disastrous marriage. The girl is a slattern: immoral, grasping and shallow. Look at the way she dresses—or undresses, rather! Didn't you see the state she was in that first night she stayed here? You saw that passionate goodnight kiss from the boatman. The boatman, Renzo!' he snapped. 'She's a walking invitation to all men, and you're merely one of the guests at the party.'

'No!'

'Yes,' he continued relentlessly, his eyes glittering with suppressed anger. 'You've been allowed to run wild for too long. Someone has to take you in hand. You don't think I enjoy this, do you? But I warn you, if you dare to soil the Mazzardi name by associating with her, then I'll make her an offer she can't refuse. *Capisci?*'

Renzo stared at his brother's menacing face in horror and realised that he was implacable in his hatred. Massimo would go to any lengths to avenge himself on the lonely years when their fiery-tempered, proud father had refused to see him—even to visit their mother. Massimo had bided his time, waiting for Father to die, and now had control of the family finances. He intended to wreak his vengeance on them all.

'I understand,' muttered Renzo with a shiver. He knew what he had to do now. Selina's sister was coming over with the money that he needed to evade Massimo and marry Selina. He had no choice. Her sister would have to be sacrificed.

CHAPTER TWO

'STRESA, *signorina*.'

Lucinda tore her mind away from home and blinked at the driver of the minibus. They were driving along the shores of a vast blue lake, backed by hazy mauve mountains. Lake Maggiore already! She groaned inwardly. What had happened to the journey? She'd been mentally going through the instructions she'd left and the daunting list of duties, in case she'd forgotten something. Had she mentioned that Mrs Knight liked a weak whisky for her bedtime drink?

Wearily she stretched her limbs, cramped from the long journey. She was the last remaining passenger; hopefully she could soon have a bath and something to eat.

It was very hot now, and her long hair hung damply down her spine. As always, she had caught it at the nape of her neck with a plain ribbon, a smoky blue like her simple V-necked dress. Now, in the brilliant and cruel sunlight, she noticed that the collar was a little threadbare.

That upset her. It was in her nature to be neat, and she had imagined that it would be ideal for facing up to Mazzardi. That left only her best blouse and skirt, more suitable for evening wear than daytime, and she'd feel conscious that it was inappropriate. Things like that were important. Lucy always worried about details. For her, everything had to be right.

The coach rolled to a stop in a large car park. Lucy consulted the piece of paper, where she'd written down

19

the name of the resort and the hotel mentioned by Selina. This wasn't the right place, not Stresa. The driver had made a mistake.

He was looking at her enquiringly. 'You, Pescatori?' he queried.

She checked the name again. 'Yes, Hotel Borromeo.'

'You get out, please.'

'But—you said this was Stresa!'

'Stresa, yes. Come.'

Lucy felt puzzled. Perhaps this was as far as the bus went. Bother! It looked as if she was going to be dropped miles from the hotel.

Reluctantly, Lucy clambered out into the burning heat. Judging by the lack of activity and the silence, it was siesta time. Across the road, tall and secretly shuttered houses slept in the noonday sun. Her mind strayed. She hoped Mrs Knight would settle for her afternoon nap. Lucy usually sat holding her hand until she did, and she doubted that the stand-in would have the time.

'*Signorina?*'

The driver's smiling, friendly face swam into view.

'Oh, sorry.' She smiled, feeling foolish. 'Where do I go?'

'Come,' he said to Lucy, beckoning. He collected her small case and ambled along with a relieved Lucy following. It looked as if he was going to show her where to pick up a bus or something. Perhaps Pescatori was the next village. At least she wouldn't be abandoned and left to fend for herself. She had quite enough on her mind as it was, without searching for backstreet hotels.

To her surprise, they bypassed a large building that appeared to be a ticket office of some kind, and turned instead on to a path beside the lake.

The view was unforgettable. Lucy stopped, transfixed. Here was her fairy-tale setting. A magical place
of gentle beauty, of softly whispering plane trees and
contrasting dark palms silhouetted against the incredible, breathtaking backdrop. The lake was as flat as
a huge piece of blue stained glass and as deep in colour.
On it were tiny little islands, three of them set like care-
lessly dropped emeralds, lush with vegetation. The fourth
was a delight to the eye, crammed with tall tile-topped
buildings in every shade of ochre.

From distant pine-clad shores, a passenger-ferry was
setting out, bound for one of the islands. Nothing else
disturbed the glassy surface of the lake.

Dazed, her face relaxed and happy, she turned slowly
to see that the driver had put her case down some distance away and was returning to her.

'Boat. You go.'

Lucy looked at the motor-boats, moored to the sloping
stone of the man-made banks. 'Me? You want me to
take one of those?' She looked across the lake where a
town nestled cosily in a bay. How lovely, if that was
Pescatori!

'*Si*. Pescatori. Boat.' The driver waved a plump arm
at the launches and she realised they must be water-taxis.
'Have a nice holiday!'

She beamed at him. Such a wonderful way to arrive!
'Goodbye, thank you,' she said. The driver kissed his
fingers at her, said something she didn't understand and
hurried off. Lucy walked towards her case, examining
the launches moving imperceptibly on the crystal-clear
water.

All the boatmen seemed to be asleep! Lucy hesitated
to wake them. She glanced at her watch. Maybe it was
their lunch hour. Allowing for the difference in time,

Mrs Baker would be just about falling asleep over her pudding. A pang of homesickness hit her.

Slowly she strolled along, wondering what to do. Perhaps she ought to take up Lionel's method of attracting attention abroad. She shrank from standing on the quayside and yelling, though! It wasn't her style.

A movement caught her eye. Further up, a little distance from the other water-taxis, was one which was rocking as though someone had recently boarded it. She hurried along to see.

'Hello?' she called uncertainly.

The man at the wheel in the peaked cap appeared not to hear. He was gunning the engine now, and Lucy panicked in case he drove away without her.

'Hey!'

The man took no notice. He must lose a lot of fares by not being on the look-out! Lucy hurried along the pontoon beside the bucking boat and into his line of vision. She sighed. It would have to be Lionel's method, after all.

'Pescatori, please!' she yelled, out of breath in the dry heat.

There was a small movement of the man's head, and she found his dark eyes resting thoughtfully on her for several breathtaking seconds before he turned his attention back to the spluttering engine.

Lucy shakily set down her bag. A strange feeling of recognition had flowed through her, as if she'd known this boatman long ago—though she hadn't, of course. Confused, she grasped the boat-rail and was suddenly half lifted from her feet as the launch responded to the throttle.

In a flash, the man had switched off the engine and caught her in his strong, crushing arms before her legs were trapped between the boat and the pontoon.

Lucy found herself on board, still in the circle of his arms. One of his hands had strayed to touch her hair. She pulled herself away, still shaking.

'That was pretty stupid.' His throaty voice, the calm gaze of his deep, lustrous brown eyes, made Lucy feel as if she'd been thrown off balance.

'I was only trying to get on board,' she said, every inch of her dainty body stiff with indignance.

'What for?'

Cheeky man! The long tourist season had evidently been too much for his temper. He was certainly an old hand, because his English was good, with barely any accent at all. He was poor, though. She had noticed that he was barefoot, his long, tanned legs disappearing into rather brief and disreputably ragged black shorts, shiny with oil. His T-shirt, also black, was similarly glistening with streaks of oil. She looked at his hands. Oil! In dismay, she tried to check the back of her dress where he had touched her.

He spun her around. 'A little oil is better than breaking your ribs and getting soaked as well. It'll wash out,' he said huskily.

Lucy's mouth thinned. He didn't know much about stains! She couldn't afford to mess up her clothes like that.

'You shouldn't have revved up the engine like that,' she said accusingly.

'I don't need permission from you,' he said quietly.

'You ought to have been watching the pontoon!'

'Why?' came the infuriating answer. 'In case an idiot woman decided to commit suicide?'

Irritated with his arrogant backchat, she let her impatience show. 'Just take me to Pescatori,' she snapped.

He didn't move, his disconcerting gaze steadily boring into her head in a singularly personal way. The sharp jawline tightened.

'Why the hell should I?' he murmured, a slight growl of annoyance in his tone.

'Because I'm tired and hot and hungry, and I want to have a bath and a meal.' She flicked a glance at the other water-taxis. Maybe it would be wiser to get off this boat and wake up a more willing—and less insolent—boatman.

When he didn't answer, Lucy tipped up her head to glare at him and saw to her astonishment that a small smile was playing about his strong, masculine mouth. His lips were curling expressively and then he was grinning at her, his perfect white teeth suddenly parting as a series of chuckles came from deep within his chest.

Uncertainly, well out of her depth with the unorthodox Italian, she stared back, her big hazel eyes wide with suspicion.

'Forgive me,' he said softly, inclining his head for a brief moment. 'The engine needs a little further coaxing and then I am at your service.'

He indicated the leather seat behind her and she sat cautiously among the bright cushions while he fetched her case and continued his adjustments to the panel by the steering wheel.

The mollified Lucy sat on the edge of the seat like a dainty little bird poised for flight. A vague feeling of unease nagged at her and she pushed it aside, knowing that it was up to her to plan the next few hours to the best advantage. Presumably Selina was working and would meet her at the hotel that evening. So if she freshened up...

Her beautiful soft eyes rested absently on the boatman, distracted by the sheen of smooth, satin skin on his arms. As he worked, his biceps swelled beneath the short sleeves and muscles under the dauntingly broad back shifted in a fascinating way. He'd planted his legs firmly apart for balance, and she was idly examining their tautness when she discovered to her confusion that he had turned around.

Flustered, she blinked up at him to be rocked by his imprisoning eyes, this time sensually and meticulously checking her over, inch by inch, his thick fringe of black lashes dropping on to the taut skin of his high cheekbones as his impertinent scrutiny reached her cheap sandals.

Lucy had blushed when his eyes paused at the sight of her frayed collar. Her flush had deepened even more when his gaze stopped on her breasts, and then humiliation ran through her when she realised his total lack of interest in her body, and that his attention had been arrested by the carefully darned buttonhole.

'I can pay the fare,' she said haughtily, on the defensive.

His slow, deliberate examination was taking in her small, work-worn fingers with their short, unpolished nails. Her small chin jutted out. She had nothing to be ashamed of.

'There is no fare,' he said unexpectedly.

'Don't patronise me! I can pay my way.' She tossed her head, and to her irritation the ribbon slipped under the weight of her hair, releasing cascades of bright waves over her shoulders.

'Time, I think, to cast off,' he murmured, almost to himself.

With deft fingers, she gathered up every strand and tied the ribbon with angry movements.

'Are you comfortable?' he asked, amused.

No, she definitely was not comfortable! 'Just go,' she said, cross and tired, almost at the end of her tether. Oddly behaving boatmen hadn't come into her plans at all.

'I am sorry,' he said, manoeuvring the launch out of the harbour. He kept one hand on the wheel, the other in his pocket, with his body half turned to her. She wished he would give his whole attention to driving the boat! 'I've never done this kind of thing before,' he added disarmingly.

'Oh!' A rush of understanding and sympathy filled Lucy, and she smiled slightly at him. 'Your first time? she asked warmly.

'My first time,' he said solemnly.

He opened up the throttle and the water churned behind them in curling white waves, disturbing the glasslike surface. Lucy settled back against the cushions. Sumptuous cushions. Of course, now she looked, it was a new boat. The woodwork was unmarked by use and the chrome rails gleamed without a trace of rust.

'I wish you every success,' she said generously, surprising herself. It wasn't in her nature to be impulsive.

She was treated to a flash of his white teeth. 'Thank you. I wish you success, too, in your life.'

'I'll need it,' she sighed, her face falling.

The black lashes hid his eyes. 'A young girl like you should have no worries.'

'Tell my worries that,' she said bitterly.

He tilted back his peaked cap to reveal a cluster of black Botticelli curls, pressed damply on his forehead.

'Pescatori will make you forget all your troubles,' he promised.

Lucy could well believe that. From the town, there must be a wonderful view of the islands. They seemed so serene and peaceful that it looked like they were floating on a mirror. Her serious expression disappeared and a slow, dreamy look spread over her face; Lucy's irresistible madonna smile. The boat was moving very slowly, almost drifting. It was a magical journey, one she would remember all her life.

He was staring, she knew. When he spoke next, it was in such a low-pitched voice that something about its resonance echoed deep inside Lucy, startling her with its intensity.

'Beautiful.'

'And I never knew they existed,' she sighed wistfully.

'Ah, the islands!' He smiled. 'You know nothing about our Borromean Islands?'

She feasted her eyes on the long narrow one, every inch apparently packed with houses. Soaring from their midst was the long slender spire of a church, piercing the deep blue sky.

'Nothing at all,' she confessed softly. 'It's like a make-believe world to me.'

A brief, cynical expression twisted his beautiful mouth. 'It's real enough. People here still live, die, argue, hate and make love, as they do in the rest of the world.' He took off his cap and threw it on to the seat, lifting his head to the slight breeze. Lucy felt her throat constrict at the pure lines of his profile. He was an extraordinarily handsome man. 'And you,' he continued more gently, 'are you joining a lover, or merely looking for one?'

The word had been caressed by his lips as he spoke it
in his unusual husky voice. Her breath had been stopped
for a moment, and her head spun giddily with the un-
intentional compliment. He'd automatically assumed
that she had lovers; that she was interesting and attractive enough physically! The idea made her glow
inside. After all, men had only been briefly interested in
her. When they discovered she came complete with a
Rest Home and ten dependents, they backed out smartly.
Lucy had long ago abandoned socialising. No man would
want to take on her responsibilities.

'Do I look the kind of woman who takes a holiday in
order to find a lover?' she asked sharply. There was hurt
in her expression. Part of the romance had gone from
the situation. He'd reminded her that her chosen life
brought spinsterhood with it.

His eyes were compassionate. 'No. In fact, you look
too good to be true,' he admitted. 'Like a miniature
angel, plucked from heaven, basking in sunbeams. May
I ask a personal question?'

She blinked, still digesting his words. Italian boatmen
were incurably romantic!

'Is that your natural hair colour?' he asked.

Lucy grinned. 'No one in their right mind would dye
their hair orange,' she declared.

'Orange?'

'Carrots. Ginger,' she supplied, recalling how she'd
been teased as a child at school.

'Amber,' he said firmly. 'Known to the ancient world
as electron. It attracts things, you know, especially when
stroked. Like a magnet,' he added helpfully.

Lucy was well aware that he was flirting, and she dis-
approved, despite the glow within her. Amber! How
cleverly seductive.

'It traps unsuspecting creatures, too,' he murmured, his compelling eyes trapping *her* with their smouldering intensity. 'Holds them fast, forever.' His approach was highly successful, however much she resisted it. She felt breathless from the impact of his sensuality and the sheer virility pouring from his bronzed body.

Such relentlessness either deserved a prize or a put-down! Wisely she decided on the latter.

'Sounds dangerous, and to be avoided at all costs.'

'Danger can be thrilling,' he murmured. 'Stimulating.'

'Shouldn't you be looking where you're going?' she asked with unaccustomed asperity.

'I thought I was.' He smiled pleasantly.

For one mad moment, Lucy wanted to return that open, honest smile. What a pity convention demanded that she didn't let strange men flirt with her! It really was a very good feeling.

'No. You were mistaken. You were a long way off course.'

Putting on one of her stony expressions, she deliberately shifted her body so that she couldn't see him any longer and earnestly stared at the view. One of those islands must be where Selina was working, the one owned by Mazzardi. She considered asking the boatman which one it was, then decided not to arouse any curiosity. Remembering her task, she had begun to frown. Her fingers thoughtfully touched her neat arched mouth and her eyes grew turbulent.

A rising of the hairs on the back of her neck alerted her to the man's continued attention. The intensity of his interest invaded her thoughts and she felt increasingly uncomfortable. The tension he was unwittingly creating needed to be broken, somehow. It was telling on her nerves.

As if moving in slow motion, she forced her head around casually, proving to herself that she could talk to him as normally as she might to a seventy-year-old man. 'Is it far to Pescatori?' she asked in an offhand tone. They were quite a way from the shore still, and the boat was moving at an infuriatingly slow speed. Lucy wondered if there was a speed limit on the lake.

He studied her for a few long seconds before answering, his eyes conveying a confusing mixture of admiration and considerable interest, while the virile way he stood produced only one message: raw, feasting sexuality. Intuitively, Lucy knew from the kind of man he was, from the unrestrained animal power emanating earthily from his very skin, that he was at ease with women, and confident in his own ability to master them and conquer their inhibitions. He represented the kind of men she disliked: shallow, grasping, hedonistic men who didn't respect women at all. A sensualist, she thought wildly, her body aflame from the openly carnal invitation. She should have been offended, scandalised, even. Any other man projecting that elemental hunger would have made her ice up in a frigid response, and she had no idea why he was different. But he was. Every fibre of her being quivered at his power to attract.

'Pes——' She cleared her throat. 'Pescatori?'

'The island,' he said very gently, as if wary of making her shy away, 'is not far. Judge for yourself.'

'Island?' she repeated stupidly, emerging from the fog she'd been immersed in.

'Yes. Isola dei Pescatori, Fisherman's Island. That's where you wanted to go, wasn't it?'

'You mean——?' Her delighted face searched his for confirmation and she melted at the charming, curling smile which destroyed her defences and made her forget any sensible caution as far as he was concerned. 'I don't believe it! It's an island? This one, with the houses? Oh, that's just wonderful. I had no idea!' She sat forwards, intent and eager, her body alerted, two huge, glistening eyes riveted on the nearby island he'd nodded to with his dark, handsome head. 'How perfect, to stay on a tiny magical island, in the middle of a lake...!'

Words failed her. She clutched the edge of the seat tightly, her mind whirling, forced to discard the idea she'd formed in her head originally of her hotel: a small room in a third-grade dive in the middle of a noisy town. It was incredibly thoughtful of Selina to find such an idyllic spot! How sweet of her, amid all her troubles!

Unaware that her face shone with a luminous inner glow and that her eyes sparkled like bright stars, she laughed aloud in sheer exhilaration and pleasure, perfect neat pearly teeth set off by the natural rose of her happily curving lips. The amber strands of her hair fanned out behind her like long, glistening threads. Her slender body, honed by years of hard work, strained forwards eagerly, the small, high breasts suddenly evident in the thinly stretched cotton dress.

'I hope Pescatori lives up to your expectations,' said the man huskily. 'And that you experience... pleasure.'

'I'm here on business.' She sighed sadly. The beauty of her surroundings dimmed a little at the reminder.

'On Pescatori?'

'Partly.' Strangely, she felt reluctant to be so reticent, longing to pour out the whole story to him. He had a listening quality, a receptiveness that made her want to confide in him. But she must be careful, for Selina's sake. The matter was private.

His dark brow winged upwards. 'Business? And yet you didn't even know where you were going.'

Lucy cautiously met his liquid eyes and gulped at the way they saw into her soul and all her worries. Seconds stretched into an eternity. The engine stopped and a tide of feeling rose within her. She ought to snap something witty at him, but didn't think her voice would get past the lump in her throat.

'Madonna!' She barely heard the word, it was said so quietly. He shook his head slowly and took a deep breath, stretching the thin T-shirt across his big ribcage. A perplexed look drew his straight black brows together.

'Why have you stopped?' she asked in a croak.

'Perhaps the boat is bewitched, like me,' he said slowly. 'Have you ever done anything unexpected, unwise, even?' he asked.

'No, of course not,' she replied with difficulty.

He seemed to smile. 'Neither have I. Ever wanted to?'

Yes, she thought fervently. Oh, yes. She wanted to, right at this moment! She wanted to invite him to sit next to her and tell her all about himself. He held a world of knowing behind those dark pooling eyes!

'Sometimes,' she answered, her voice higher pitched than usual.

'Me too,' he said shakily. 'But I've never given in, never lost control. All my life I've considered every action and its likely results. But ... once in a lifetime, lightning strikes, breaking down walls, barriers ... Do you understand what I am saying?'

'Your English is very good,' she said.

He frowned and Lucy flushed immediately, feeling contrite. 'I'm sorry,' she said. 'But aren't you being a little ... fast?'

'Yes, I am. Madly so. But it's that kind of situation, isn't it?'

Lucy felt the tug of his incredible charm and honesty. 'Is it?' she fended.

'Look, I must see you again,' he said seriously. 'Where are you staying? Hotel Borromeo? Will you have dinner with me tonight?' he asked gently, seeing her startled eyes.

'No, I can't. I'm meeting someone,' she said huskily, half sorry.

'Pity. Is this the lover? That's how you look, as if you're eager, breathless, expectant. Or do you always look like that?'

'Please——!' Lucy tried to think straight. 'I mustn't stay here any longer.'

'No? Wouldn't it be wonderful to stay here and never set foot on shore again?'

Her eyes dreamed for a brief moment. Wonderful. 'Very inconvenient,' she said, summoning up a matter-of-fact tone. To be released from money worries, from Selina's problems... Lucy smiled to herself. She'd miss everyone too much. But the idea of stopping the clock and staying on the boat in this romantic setting with a romantic, handsome man was utterly seductive! 'We'd get extremely hungry, for one thing.'

He chuckled. 'No problem. The fishermen would bring us food. The advantages would far outweigh the disadvantages.'

'What advantages?' she asked coolly, her heart thudding.

His eyes danced and took on the colour of molten jet. 'Being free to do as we wish. The opportunity for me to get to know you before the world spoils your gentle nature.'

Lucy didn't know how on earth to handle him. She fought against the force that was drawing them together, the appealing, believable tone as if he did truly speak from his heart. For her, it was as if there had been an instant empathy, as if she could go on knowing him for ever and yet never know him—know their compatibility, that was—any better than she did right at this moment. Despite all the doubts which her common-sense mind kept repeating, whatever strange communication which had passed between them had told her all she needed to know, and the longer they stayed with eyes locked, searching into each other's souls, the more she knew that this Italian boatman was her impossible destiny and that for the rest of her life she would probably never find such an instant, certain rapport again.

And it was ridiculous, of course. Part of the fairy-tale, the cruelly weaving magic of the lake and its little islands strung out like broken beads in a necklace. Miserably, Lucy tore her eyes from his and dropped her lashes. It was the first time she'd been let off the leash, and already she'd started fantasising! She'd been sheltered for far too long; she really ought to get out more, and then maybe she wouldn't find undying romance at every turn!

'Well?' he prompted.

She stared blindly at the water. Drifting logs, brought down by the recent torrential rains which had swollen the rivers, surrounded the launch with soft bumping sounds till it seemed as though they were on a little wooden island of their own. Was he thinking of carrying out his threat to stay on the lake, till, perhaps, she agreed to go out with him or something? She had to meet Selina! Dispirited with the unpleasant reality which faced her, she suddenly felt tired and reluctant to fight any battles or meet any problems.

'Now you're worrying again. I'm concerned about you,' he said in a concerned tone.

'You're what?' She sat bolt upright at his nerve.

'You are preoccupied about something, aren't you? Let me help you. I'm good at smoothing out difficulties.'

She studied him carefully. 'What makes you think I need help?'

He shrugged. 'You've had a faraway look in your eyes all the time. So faraway that you didn't notice that this is not a water-taxi but a private launch.'

Dawning horror spread over Lucy's face and her hand flew to her mouth.

'Private? Not—not a water-taxi at all? Oh, dear!' Flustered, she rose, looked around at the expanse of water between them and the mainland, then she groaned. No wonder he'd been offhand! 'I'm sorry, I thought——'

'I think you need my services,' he said, coming towards her. His eyes glowed with a strange light she'd never seen before.

Dear heaven, she thought wildly, he was intending something awful! 'Services? W-what do you mean?' She took a step back, felt the cushioned seat hit the back of her knee and sat down hurriedly. Instead of the expected assault, he crouched down in front of her, a kindly expression on his face. But that made it worse. He'd read all too easily what she'd been thinking of him; he knew that she was naïve and stupidly romantic, fashioning dreams from a few imaginary glances. Did he think she was longing for romance, and ready to share herself for a few charming phrases? Shame filled her eyes.

'Relax,' he said gently.

He smelt faintly of warmth and musk. No one remotely as masculine had been this close to her before. Or if they had, she'd never been so aware or nervous. It wasn't a fear she recognised; something more primitive that pulled at her inside and made her body flush with heat. She *had* to keep her mind firmly fixed on the reason she was here. How could she allow herself to be side-tracked so easily? It was important for her to escape this man's attentions. Lines furrowed her brow. There was nowhere for her to run and no one within hailing distance.

'You are worried about something, aren't you?' he probed, his soft, faintly moist lips fascinating Lucy.

With an effort she concentrated on answering him, trying to overcome her turgid mind. Her body felt as if it was flowing, swaying imperceptibly towards his hypnotic eyes, her lips softening like his and pouting forwards. His lashes swept down on his cheekbones, and she knew he had sensed that slight movement of her mouth and was responding with his own parted lips. The tip of his tongue touched pinkly between his even white teeth, and she drew in air through her own teeth, drawing in with that breath the warm, somnolent atmosphere and his man-smell.

'Yes. I'm very worried about getting to the hotel in time for my appointment,' she lied in a slightly breathless voice. It was all she could think of on the spur of the moment. It was essential that she somehow broke the spell that was being cast over her, here on this water paradise. If she didn't get hold of herself, she'd end up looking and acting like a fool over this man. He was no doubt used to that; but she was hardly in a position to moon over an itinerant Romeo, with her sister in danger.

Emotional exhaustion was beginning to make her body sag again. 'I'm sorry I made the mistake about your boat,' she continued wearily, 'but you could easily have told me. I see why you were amused. However, since you got me out here, you are under an obligation to darn well finish the trip. And please hurry. I'm really tired.'

'What a strange mixture you are,' he smiled. 'Dreamy, worried, sharp, soft, receptive, beautifully inno-cent——'

Her eyes blazed. This was the most extraordinary conversation she'd ever had in her life! Why this assessment of her as 'innocent' should annoy her so much she didn't know; it made her feel gauche and stupid in his eyes, and she was wishing idiotically that he'd think she was a woman not to be trifled with.

'My character is not open for discussion. I resent your ridiculous assessment,' she said tightly and a little pompously, pushed beyond endurance. 'To be frank, I find your behaviour offensive. I'm firmly resisting the temptation to stick my foot in your chest and heave, but I can't guarantee my patience won't run out at any moment. I am preoccupied and not in the best of moods, so cut out the chat. You might be bored, and enjoying spending time picking up young women and pestering them, but I have things to do.'

Instead of responding angrily, he gave a slow grin.

'Usually people find the scenery improves their outlook on life. Lakes are supposed to be very restful, though I seem to remember that psychiatrists link them with sex. What do you think?'

'I think,' she said, her teeth grinding together in frustrated rage, 'that you've stepped out of line and are asking for your face to be slapped.'

'Ah, contact at last,' he mused, with a pleased chuckle and an appealing grin.

In fact, it was so appealing that Lucy felt her mouth quirking at the edges, and this infuriated her so much that she over-reacted and cracked her hand across the high golden cheekbone and the dark hollow underneath.

Appalled, she drew her hand slowly back, retaining a vivid impression of the satin feel of his skin, its warmth and the strength of the bones beneath. She clutched at her hand as if to deny that it had ever committed such an uncontrolled deed.

'I'm sorry!'

He had rocked on his heels, briefly dropping a hand to steady himself, but remained crouched in front of her, the white imprint of her fingers changing to a deep pink while he regarded her speculatively.

'Poor madonna. You *are* on edge. I think you need a bath, a drink and an hour or so gazing at the lake. You'll find that restful. After that . . . who knows what images it will conjure up for you, or what yearnings it will create?'

Lucy sighed in relief. He was going to let her go. And he was right: she needed time to adjust and get a bit of peace and quiet before Selina descended on her. Taking her silence as acquiescence, he started the engine again, steering the boat away from the driftwood and then accelerating so rapidly that she was pressed back into the seat and had to hang on grimly as he swung the boat around in a huge curve which cut across the wash from a large ferry. She tried to push the incident out of her mind. Her nerves were frayed, and it was his fault that he'd gone too far. That probably wasn't the first slap he'd had, even if it was the first time she'd delivered one!

The faint strains of a lilting song came from his direction, and she made an effort to ignore him. But she thought of him, nevertheless, remembering details like the way the sun caught dark hairs on his arms, how neat and clean his nails were and how strongly his brows sprang above his eyes. Guiltily she struggled to plan her meeting with Selina.

Isola dei Pescatori looked even more intriguing close up, its houses packed so tightly that she wondered how they'd ever built the last one. A line of plane trees ran along a narrow point at one end, and beneath them she could see huge stacks of neatly piled wood. There was a minute harbour with canvas-covered fishing-boats and a small jetty. Her spirits rose again at the prospect of exploring.

As they approached, Lucy saw a number of water-taxis, their hulls wedged on the gently sloping bank. In a moment they were alongside, with a grinding sound as the bottom of the boat was driven hard on to the stone. The journey was over. Her moment of magic had passed. She bit her lip. 'How much?' she mumbled without looking at him. It seemed indecent to ask.

'Nothing.'

His voice was deeply husky and she did look up then, with a quick frown of annoyance. 'I said, how much?'

'I would appreciate a kiss,' he murmured.

'Then you'll have to make do with nothing,' she said shakily.

He seemed pleased with her answer. 'I'll collect later,' he laughed gently.

'I think not.' She picked up her case, deeply offended and unaccountably disturbed.

He took it from her, helped her off with practised grace, and handed it back.

'Thanks.'

'Not at all,' he answered solemnly, quite unaffected by her sharpness. It would be water off a duck's back, she thought wryly. Why should he care if his little game with a shabby tourist backfired? 'The hotel is along the path to the right,' he added. 'Enjoy your bath. I'll be thinking of you.' He chuckled at her furious glare. 'You are so serious! Let go a little! And try not to miss the beauty of the lake. Remember what it signifies.'

His eyes captured hers, his gaze lingering too long. Lucy knew she must look stupid, standing there transfixed, but it really did take an effort of will before she was able to look away. It seemed that the fishermen around were surprised at her rather obvious behaviour, too, because they were staring at her in curiosity and nodded and beamed at her; hardly stopping in their examination of their nets which slid rapidly through their skilful fingers.

'I'll be seeing you,' called a warm, masculine voice.

'Not if I see you first,' she said sharply.

His delighted laugh was drowned as the powerful engines throbbed, and with a sigh of relief Lucy began to walk along the narrow path towards the hotel.

CHAPTER THREE

'SELINA!' Lucy dropped her case in the hotel's little hall as a deeply tanned blonde vision rose from a bench and flew into her arms. Despite the fact that she was a good six inches shorter, Lucy immediately felt protective and was ready to defend her against harm.

'You're so late!' complained Selina. 'I've been waiting ages.'

'But you said . . .'

'Change of plan. Get your key and let's go and talk,' she urged.

Lucy hurriedly checked in and waited while the manager consulted his list of room allocations.

'Aren't you supposed to be at work?' she queried, looking at her half-sister sternly. It wouldn't do if she was sacked and had no income.

'I'll have to plead sickness or something. This is more important than work. I thought I'd have time to see you in my lunch hour, but you've taken far too long! What have you been up to? You're not supposed to be sight-seeing, you know.'

Guilt washed over her. The boat journey could have been done in half the time. 'You said you weren't coming round till after dinner,' reminded Lucy, mildly irritated, flashing the manager a brief smile as he handed over the room key. She hadn't known Selina would be cooling her heels.

'I know. I couldn't wait. They'll have to cope without me. Oh, do come on, there's so little time!'

Lucy was being rushed again and didn't like it. So much had happened since yesterday morning; enough excitement and drama to last her a lifetime. She forgave Selina for being illogical, though, because she was evidently distraught under her bright make-up and casual manner.

'Look, you ought to go back to your job before they miss you,' she said quietly. 'Besides, I'm not ready to talk. I'm tired, I've had a lot to do.'

'*You've* had a lot to do? What about me? You've no idea what I've gone through, worrying about prison and being bumped off.' Selina pushed her sister towards the stairs and hailed a passing waiter at the same time. '*Due* brandies, *molto grande*. Or is it *mucho*?' she said to herself, wrinkling her dark golden brow. 'Big brandies. Yes?'

The waiter smiled, his eyes trying not to stray to Selina's heaving bosom in the low-cut sundress.

'I can't tell you what hell it's been!' she groaned, whirling Lucy upwards.

'I haven't eaten for ages, I don't want a brandy, I——'

'Don't worry. I could drink them both,' said Selina reassuringly. 'This is your room.'

Resigned, she let Selina take the key and show her in to the darkened room. She sank to the bed and kicked off her plain chain-store sandals, rubbing the sore places on her toes. If only she'd had time to buy a new pair of shoes... Darn it, if only she wasn't here! The old familiar whirlwind around Selina had taken her over and was blowing her in whatever direction Selina fancied.

'You unpack and I'll talk,' said Selina, throwing open the floor-length green shutters and flooding the room with sunshine.

For once, Lucy ignored her, drinking in the simple
Italianate surroundings. It was a large, airy room graced
by a massive wardrobe, big enough to hide a family, and
an enormous double bed with an ornate wrought-iron
hand-painted bedhead. The coverlet looked like something out of an English stately home, all thick-cut velvet
in an inky blue and with fancy trailing tassels. There was
an impossibly elaborate carved chaise-longue in gilded
wood and upholstered in gold satin, and an elegant,
spindly ebony chair. And through the shutters she could
see a red-tiled terrace and a stunning view of the lake
and two islands.

'Lulu! Don't go out there,' wailed Selina, dramati-
cally barring her eyes with a theatrical arm. 'I couldn't
bear to look at it!'

'Look at what?' she asked, exasperated. Selina had
taken to Italian overstatement like a duck to water!

'The island. The one with all the woods and flowers
and that massive palace. That's where I work.'

Lucy padded out, the tiles hot to her bare feet, feeling
like a queen at having a balcony of her own. Dear Selina.
She alone knew what a romantic nature lay underneath
Lucy's practical exterior. Steps ran down from the
balcony to a narrow sliver of rock at the water's edge.
Her own secret place to bathe! The island was too
photogenic to be true. A large, uncompromisingly square
building rose from a sea of greenery which cascaded
down simple stone terraces to the deep blue lake. Splashes
of red and purple suggested that the gardens were full
of geraniums and bougainvillaea.

She remembered Selina with guilt and returned to the
room. 'Looks gorgeous, your island.'

'It's deadly.'

She contemplated the dispirited girl. 'What exactly have you done?' she asked seriously.

'Stop glaring. Can't you unpack or something? It's too difficult to explain with you looking at me like mean, menacing Mazzardi.'

'Like what?' Lucy shot her sister a look of amusement.

'Oh, you can laugh, but he takes himself seriously,' said Selina glumly.

Resisting the temptation to probe further, Lucy busied herself. All in good time: Selina's good time.

'Perhaps you'd begin by drawing the picture for me,' she suggested, taking over her one cotton dress and the blouse and skirt to hang in the wardrobe.

'Is that all you brought?' Selina came over and fingered them in dismay.

'Don't worry, you won't have to be seen in public with me,' said Lucy wryly. 'And get your hands out of my case now.'

'These aren't suitable——' Selina chewed at her lip. 'Haven't you anything more stylish?'

'I wasn't intending to wangle an invitation to one of Mazzardi's masked balls,' she said mildly. 'My best blouse and skirt will do for here. I brought another shirt.' She studied Selina's eye-boggling dress. 'You don't wear that for work, do you? I should think it would stop everyone in their tracks!'

'It does, a bit,' laughed Selina. 'No, I changed before I came over on the ferry. The uniform I wear is foul—terribly prim and boring. If I undo as much as a button I get snarled at by old Mazzardi.'

'So you wear a uniform and get snarled at a lot. What else does this job entail?' smiled Lucy.

'Oh, it's heaven seeing you again,' sighed Selina, putting her arms around Lucy and giving her a hug. 'You treat me like a real person. That's rare.' She giggled at Lucy's mocking glance at her generous cleavage. 'I know, I know. I feel so confined in the uniform. Well, you'd like my job. I'm one of the English guides for the Mazzardi *palazzo*. It's incredibly dull. Just your sort of thing. I would have left after the first day if I hadn't met Renzo.'

'Renzo?' She waited patiently, letting in the waiter and handing both brandies to Selina.

'Oh, put it on the bill. The *conto*,' she said absently to the waiter.

Lucy tried not to worry. A couple of drinks weren't going to make too big a dent in her money, and it looked as though Selina would erupt if she objected. Her half-sister was really upset. Once she'd begun to talk about her job and Renzo, her face had fallen into anxious lines and her eyes showed desperation. Her hands were trembling too, making the drink swirl in the glasses.

'That's better,' breathed Selina, taking a huge gulp. 'Mazzardi owns the island. Renzo is his younger brother. It's a terribly old family and their ancestors are all lined up and glaring at me from the walls of every room I go in. The *palazzo* over there must be worth a cool fortune with all the contents.'

'And Renzo?' Lucy sensed he had something to do with Selina's troubles.

'I'm in love with him—don't look so startled, I know it's a bit quick, but you can fall for someone at first sight, really.'

Yesterday Lucy wouldn't have understood. Today was different. If he had any of the magnetism of the man who had momentarily turned her head out there on the lovely lake, Renzo could well have fascinated Selina.

'In fact,' she was saying shyly, 'he's bought me a ring. Look.'

It was enormous, a chunky diamond, glittering wickedly on Selina's finger. It was astonishing she hadn't noticed it before; it must have cost a great deal.

'I hadn't realised you were actually engaged,' she said slowly. 'That was a bit hasty, love. How well can you know someone in such a short time? Have you thought this out? It's not one of your virtues, is it, thinking things through? You need a great deal in common as well as love. That isn't enough on its own.'

'You haven't mentioned our different backgrounds.' Selina's mouth was sulky.

'No. That doesn't matter too much if everything else is right. And weren't you saying that Renzo's brother was evil? I don't understand——'

'He's foul! Massimo has always resented Renzo. Lulu, darling, that's where you come in. With your nice ways and maiden aunt manner, he'll listen to you.'

'Thanks,' muttered Lucy.

'Well, it's true.' Selina tossed her curls. 'He disapproves of me and thinks I'm a gold-digger. Unfortunately he controls the family purse, and without his approval Renzo will have no money and no home. I even tried to make Massimo accept me by seducing Renzo, but the sweet darling was shocked and said his bride must be a virgin on her wedding night.'

Lucy dropped the shoe she was holding. 'Do you mean...' Her voice died away in disbelief. Selina had gained quite a reputation with the boys and young men at home.

'I liked a good time, but not that good a time,' said Selina in embarrassment. 'That's why they got so aggressive. I am a virgin and I'm glad. But Renzo and I can't wait. We want each other so much and it's driving us mad. We must marry.'

'It sounds as if you need a long engagement to sort out your suitability. I'll come over with you tomorrow and talk to Mazzardi,' said Lucy comfortingly.

'No!' Selina took hold of her shoulders, her face distorted, her fingernails digging in painfully. 'I want to marry Renzo now. I must, before Mazzardi gets rid of me.'

'In what way? Gently, love. What are you afraid of?'

With a moan, Selina threw herself on the bed and began to sob hysterically, calming down a little when Lucy sat down beside her and held her tightly, soothing and stroking.

'He's foul! A snob! He called me a tart! He said he'd seen me after a disgusting assignation with one of his boatmen. Lulu, it wasn't my fault the man wanted more than to hold my hand—I had to fight him off, and ended up in an awful mess. But Mazzardi wouldn't listen to my story.'

'He'll listen to me!' Lucy cried, enraged on Selina's behalf. 'I'll definitely go and sort him out. If he thinks——'

'Do what you like, but you must see we need money to go away. I'm sure I could persuade Renzo to make love to me, and then he'd be honour-bound to marry me and Mazzardi would have to lump it.'

'That's not the way,' said Lucy gently. 'Not by deceit.'

'It's the only way! I was relying on you. You don't know what it's like to lie awake, aching for a man! Wait till you do, then you'll understand!'

Blanching from the unintended hurt, Lucy hugged the distraught girl.

'Does Renzo's brother want you for himself?' she asked, voicing her theory.

'What? No, he's made of stone. Cut me dead when I winked at him first time I bumped into him.'

'Selina!'

'Well,' she defended, 'he's an eyeful. But Renzo's sweet. No wonder everyone loves him and the family threw Massimo out.'

Lucy didn't allow herself to be sidetracked. 'You brought me over here to hand over cash for your elopement and to go and plead your case to some Italian potentate who's evil, snarls, is cold and has somehow earned everyone's hatred.'

'Something like that.'

'Oh, Selina!'

Lucy tried to gather her thoughts together. They'd both abandoned any pretence that Selina was going back to work. Lucy put away the rest of her few bits and pieces. All through her bath they talked, and afterwards, sitting together on the vast bed, with Lucy still in her housecoat, she tried to make Selina see that she ought to win Renzo's brother around by charm and persuasion.

'I'm sure Mazzardi will listen to reason if we approach him sensibly,' coaxed Lucy, after what seemed hours of talking. Night had fallen outside and they didn't seem any further towards agreement. She was weak with hunger, but wanted to clear up the major problem in private. She and Selina could eat later.

'You don't understand,' said Selina wearily. 'Renzo says Massimo never allows emotion to interfere with his life. He's violent and Renzo is afraid for my safety. We have to elope.'

'You poor darling. He sounds ghastly,' Lucy sympathised.

'You bet your life he is.'

'Nevertheless, one day won't make any difference. I'll——'

The two girls jumped at a knocking on the door. A package was handed over to Lucy. Frowning, she sat on the bed and unwrapped it. Inside was a velvet-lined jewellery box.

'There's been a mistake!' she cried, picking up the card. Then she blushed bright red.

Selina, intrigued, snatched the card from her. 'I had to see you again, I am helplessly trapped!' she read. Lucy had opened the box to reveal a beautiful amber brooch and had raised enormous troubled eyes to her sister.

The telephone rang and Lucy started.

'Oh, no!' breathed Selina. 'It's Massimo!'

'Fine,' said Lucy firmly. 'I'll have it out with him here and now. Yes?' she asked briskly.

'I like a woman who gives her answer before the question,' came a throaty voice.

'Oh! I—no, I mean——'

'I'm downstairs. I've reserved a table for us. Come and spend your first evening drinking champagne and admiring the moonlight on the water while I admire it in your eyes.'

Lucy gasped. 'No, I can't. I'm with someone.'

There was a shocked silence. 'I see,' he said tightly.

'No, you don't! It's not like that. Look, I can't accept this gift——'

'Come down and say that,' he growled.

Selina leaned closer to hear the conversation. 'What's going on?' she whispered.

Lucy rolled her eyes to heaven. She regretted her foolish fancies earlier. The boatman thought he was on to a good thing.

'I'll come down to return the brooch,' she said firmly. 'But I can't have dinner with you.' With shaking fingers she replaced the telephone. 'I won't be long,' she said, picking up the box and trying not to covet the lovely brooch. It was a very good imitation of an antique, the natural amber stone set under a tiny gilt crown. Lucy snapped the lid shut and looked around for her handbag.

'Don't rush,' muttered Selina, flopping back on the pillows. 'Let your boyfriend entertain you. I'll have a sleep. I'm whacked.'

'He's not...' Lucy gave an exasperated sigh. It wasn't worth explaining. This kind of behaviour was nothing unusual to Selina, of course. She would have taken the brooch, enjoyed the meal and said a cheery goodnight! 'Seen my bag?' she asked.

'What bag?'

Lucy gave up searching. She didn't need it really. She could put her meal on the final bill. Wherever her bag had temporarily hidden itself, it would be safe enough with Selina in the room. Quickly she slipped out of her housecoat and scrambled into her plain white blouse and the full swirling blue skirt.

'Goodness, that's prim!' muttered Selina. 'Draw the curtains, Lulu, and turn off the light. If I could have an hour's rest alone, I might see things more clearly.'

'All right. I'll get rid of this man and grab something to eat and have a walk, or something.' With swift, practised fingers, she began to draw back her hair which had been hanging loose after her bath.

'Lulu, go!'

She shot an astonished glance at Selina, who was white and shaking. 'Darling, I can't leave you like this——'

'Please! Let me think. I need to think,' she whispered.

Lucy was dismayed. Poor Selina looked as if she would snap in two at any moment. Giving her a backward glance, Lucy pushed at her hair awkwardly. It felt odd, going out with it untamed.

'You don't think badly of me, do you?' asked Selina in a choking voice.

'No, I don't,' answered Lucy, full of love. 'Everything will be OK, you'll see. Have I ever let you down?'

Selina rolled over and curled up. A worried Lucy slowly descended the stairs. He was there in the hall below, waiting in an open-neck white shirt and black linen trousers, looking impossibly handsome. Self-consciously, hoping she wouldn't trip, she moved down each step with trembling legs. His eyes scrutinised her feet in her scuffed white court shoes, her pale slender legs and gently swelling hips. In a slow, unhurried lifting of his lashes, he toured the neatly fitting blouse with its high neck and arrived at her pink, disconcerted face which glowed in the half-light. Their eyes met and Lucy came to a standstill.

He climbed the few stairs between them and reached out his hand. She placed her fingers in his, overwhelmed at the sensations chasing through her head. They had walked through the hallway and into the small rustic lounge before she reacted.

'Wait.' She pressed the jewellery box into his hand. 'I cannot accept the gift. Nor can I have dinner with you.'

To her surprise, he pocketed the box without any protest.

'Your lover objects?' he asked quietly.

She flinched. 'What kind of a world do you live in?' she asked heatedly. 'I happen to be discussing a family matter with my sister.'

He seemed uncertain. 'They've opened the champagne. Will you share a little with me?'

Lucy had the impression that he was testing her excuse and wanted him to know that she was telling the truth, that she wasn't the kind of girl who entertained lovers in her room.

'Just one drink,' she agreed.

His grin lit the dark little room. 'We make progress. Come, madonna,' he said, reaching out and taking her hand, not seeming to mind that it wasn't soft and silky.

She was glad of his confident presence as they emerged on to the open air terrace, packed with diners. It was a warm, softly black night and the busy, intimate tables glowed in candlelight.

'We have the balcony table,' he murmured. 'Over there, on the edge of the lake.'

In a half-dream at the beauty of it all, she sank into her chair, beneath a pink oleander tree, mesmerised by the flickering light on the silvered lake.

'Shall I call you madonna for ever?' He smiled.

'Lucinda,' she laughed.

'Max. To your eyes, Lucinda.' He held up his glass in salute.

'My eyes?' she exclaimed, sipping the bubbly champagne. Moët et Chandon. Real stuff, not sparkling wine. The magic was at work again!

'Careful,' murmured Max.

'Of what?' she asked nervously.

'Of being accused of theft. Shut those lovely soulful eyes of yours, quickly.'

She laughed. 'You're mad!'

'I know,' he admitted. 'No one who knew me would believe this. It's just that it looks as if you've stolen the stars from the sky and scattered them in your eyes. It's very effective,' said Max.

'I think I ought to go,' she said reluctantly, putting down her glass. He was getting too intense and it unnerved her, especially as she welcomed it so very, very much. Flattery gave her a wonderful boost!

'Ask your sister to join us,' he suggested.

'No, she wants to rest.' Darn! Her honesty had ruined her excuse to avoid dinner with him.

His finger tipped up her chin so that she was forced to look at him. 'Do you dislike me, Lucinda?' he asked gently.

She shook her head, and with a satisfied nod he turned slightly, immediately catching a waiter's eye.

'Have a look at the menu,' coaxed Max. 'The pasta is out of this world.'

So were the prices, she thought, when she looked, and her lips parted in dismay. He'd already spent a fortune on the champagne in a lovely, romantic gesture guaranteed to delight and impress her. He didn't seem to realise that it wasn't necessary.

'Max, I think I'll just have a starter, if you don't mind.'

A mixture of amusement and gentle reproach showed in his expression.

'Aren't you going to help me celebrate? I've been . . . saving up for this for a long time.'

'Celebrate? Is it your birthday? It's mine soon!'

'No. Well, perhaps it is,' he said enigmatically. 'In any case, I've found something I thought I'd lost,' he grinned. 'Something precious and rare.'

'A family heirloom?' Lucy couldn't imagine how he'd have anything valuable otherwise.

Max considered for a moment. 'Yes. You could say that.'

She beamed. 'All right, if you're sure...'

She faltered at the intense light in his eyes and her hand was suddenly captured in a fierce grip.

'To hell with the stars,' muttered Max. 'Can't you feel the sun breaking out?'

Sun? she thought wildly, her heart thudding hard; all she felt was that she was on the edge of an abyss, where one leap would take her away from her safe, known world.

'Please don't,' she whispered urgently.

Reluctantly he withdrew his hand. 'The trouble is, I know what I want and you don't,' he said in his soft, husky voice.

'Oh, yes, I do. *Zuppa verdura* with fish—perhaps the *lavaret* to follow,' she said, her neat finger following the English translation.

His eyes twinkled merrily. She'd broken the tension. Again, a brief movement from him brought the waiter hurrying over. So, others recognised his innate power, she thought. As he ordered, she cast quick glances at him from under her lashes. If his face hadn't been set in happy, relaxed lines, he would have looked quite satanic. The flickering candle had the effect of deepening the shadows beneath the high jutting cheekbones, and his neatly brushed hair, brows and lashes were as black as jet. And the night had turned his deep brown eyes to black satin. No wonder the other diners stared. She wanted to drink in his strong male features, too.

Bells began to ring from across the lake, and Lucinda looked in delight towards Mazzardi's floodlit island. Gradually she realised they were playing a tune: 'Ave Maria'. Enraptured, she clasped her small, work-lined hands together and listened till the last notes died away, melting into the darkness.

Max was sitting as still as a statue, watching her. He leaned forwards and took her hands in his, examining them, not at all disconcerted when the waiter muttered his apologies for disturbing them and skilfully slid their plates of soup under their arms. Lucy was blushing and glad the light was dim.

'Are you intending to let me starve?' she asked lightly.

He released her with an amused shake of his head. 'You do a lot of washing up.'

She sighed and spread out her left hand, seeing its roughness despite her occasional attacks with hand cream. 'I do a *mountain* of washing up,' she agreed.

'Your job?'

'I run a Rest Home.' Lucy knew this would ensure the madness ended and that he would take fright. 'I spend my life looking after my parents and eight elderly ladies.'

'Your parents can't be very old.'

'My father died in a train accident before I was born. Mother married again when I was a year old. Lionel, my stepfather, is a darling. He was in his mid-fifties then, and physically frail now. Mother has crippling arthritis.'

'And you look after all these people, you and your sister,' said Max, admiration in his voice.

She looked up, startled. 'No. Just me and a daily and a visiting physiotherapist.'

'Who's holding the fort now?' he asked with a frown. 'That kind of responsibility can't be lightly put aside.'

'You're so right!' she said with a heartfelt sigh. 'I found an emergency stand-in.'

'Emergency? Something serious?'

'No,' she hesitated, her innately cautious nature holding her back from confiding fully. It was Selina's business, after all. 'I had to get away for a couple of days.'

'I understand. That kind of work uses up a great deal of emotional energy. Why doesn't your sister help?'

'Heavens, she'd be hopeless! She's an exotic hibiscus and I'm your common or garden dandelion!'

He smiled at her description. 'I think you are like the anemone: hiding incredible beauty in a safe, unfrequented place. Have you ever looked closely at the flower?'

'Of course I have,' she said shakily. 'Have you?' He was far too male to stroll through woods peering an anemones, she thought!

'I have,' he answered solemnly. 'It has a slender stem, pearly petals and...' he smiled to himself at some private thought '...a centre of pure gold.'

'You'd never say that if you'd seen me peeling potatoes and scrubbing the kitchen floor,' grinned Lucy.

'I might. You work hard.' He touched her roughened hands again and prevented her from snatching them away. 'Don't, Lucinda. They're nothing to be ashamed of. Each line stands for your unselfish nature. Unlike your sister's. She's never helped? Don't you resent that?'

'Of course not!' she cried in surprise. Selina just wasn't cut out for that kind of work.

'Hmm. This was your chosen career?' he asked, quietly probing.

A gentle breeze stirred Lucy's loose, flowing hair and his eyes intensified in depth. She hurriedly twisted it into a less wanton-looking rope.

'I was on a horticultural course,' she confessed. 'Do you know what that is? It's——'

'I know.'

She cocked her head on one side. 'It's odd—you look Italian, but you speak English too well, with hardly a trace of accent.'

'I told you, I've only just begun to work here. Ever since I was eighteen, I lived in England.'

'Oh. So you are a boatman, after all.'

'Would that disappoint you?'

She laughed, suddenly relieved. There had been something in his manner that evening that suggested he was at ease in expensive restaurants, ordering champagne.

'No, I'd be glad. What made you come home to Italy?'

'My father died.'

His thick lashes hid his eyes, but Lucy knew from the taut jaw that he was still upset at the recent bereavement. She reached out and touched his hand in sympathy and he looked up. 'How did you make the jump from horticulture to your present career?' he asked.

He wanted to change the subject, obviously. 'I came home unexpectedly to find everything in chaos. Mum had glossed over how bad her arthritis was. She needed help, so of course I gave up the idea of landscape gardening straight away.'

'You must have hesitated.'

'No! They were my family! I love them. Wouldn't you protect and care for your family?'

He smiled a little sadly. 'Yes. Of course, if they allowed me to. Yet you made a great sacrifice.'

'Not at all. It's been incredibly rewarding and it was the right thing for me to do. We turned our big house into a Rest Home so that we could have an income. It's worked out very well. I have an affinity for the elderly.' She lowered her lashes. 'I—I'm not too keen on brash young men and parties. I can't shimmer like my sister.'

'Oh, you shimmer,' he murmured. 'As translucent as amber, as pure as gold. Many men would prefer your qualities. Especially the kind of man who is perhaps in a dark despair of his own, who needs care and solace. Someone who has found the women of the world wanting and recognises in you the purity and sweetness of an angel.'

As if he had caressed her with light fingers, she felt the skin of her body tingling in a sensitised path from the top of her head down to her feet. In an attempt to shake off the sensual languor that permeated her veins, she gave a false laugh.

'I think that poor man might be in even darker despair if he came home with me and found a roomful of elderly ladies and one elderly man!' she commented.

'Not if he valued you, he wouldn't.'

'He'd need more than that. Patience, understanding, a way with old people, tenderness—and loads of money,' she grinned.

'You can't be doing too badly, if you can manage a trip out here,' he said quietly.

She looked down. He was a local man and might gossip. Yet . . . he had only just arrived from England, and might not know Mazzardi—and she did trust him.

'I had to come. It was an emergency. It's my sister, half-sister to be accurate. She's been working over here for the last couple of weeks. There's opposition from her boyfriend's family.'

'Oh?'

Something in his tone made her flick up her eyes. He'd become wary, like an animal walking through a forest set with traps.

Confused, she stumbled on, trying to explain, realising that as an Italian he would respect family wishes.

'They want to marry and the head of the family is threatening to turn his brother out of his home and cut off his allowance. He's rather well off, you see. But Selina really loves Renzo, I know she does.'

'After a couple of weeks?' A scornful curl had arched his top lip and his eyes were bleak.

Lucy was upset that he didn't understand, and wished she'd never tried to explain. 'Whether it's a lasting love or not, they think it is and it seems heartless to oppose them without giving them a chance,' she said quietly.

'Has your sister enough experience of men to know her own mind?' he asked softly.

'Oh, yes, lots, she's had loads of boyfriends,' answered Lucy artlessly.

'Perhaps she's dazzled by this young man's wealth.'

'Most of her boyfriends were well off. That's nothing new to her.' There was a look of cold steel about his eyes suddenly. It had been a dream, then, thinking that Max was someone special. All his beautiful phrases had been empty. If he'd really been as deeply attracted to her as he said, he would have tried to understand her sister's problems. 'She's in love. Don't you believe that love can triumph over everything?' she asked defiantly, controlling her trembling lips.

'No,' he said in a low voice. 'There must be more.'

Lucy shivered at his iciness, forgetting that she had said the same thing to Selina only a short while ago. It was as if Max had withdrawn to a remote place where there was no warmth and no human life. She had to defend Selina's position.

'I know that it's difficult if people have different backgrounds. It won't be easy. But if their love is strong enough, then all that goodwill and caring takes them a long way towards a successful relationship. Don't you think so?'

'No!' he said savagely, banging down his glass of wine. 'I've just come to the conclusion that people should stay in their own worlds.'

This was turning out to be a dress rehearsal for her confrontation with Mazzardi!

'That would make us all far too insular,' she said defiantly, her face rosy with the wine and the argument. 'Nature has a way of introducing a bit of new blood into branches of the human race, whether they like it or not. Do you honestly think the Italian aristocracy would be better if they kept inter-marrying?'

That had shaken him! He'd stopped twirling his glass around angrily and was frozen into immobility. She must remember that line tomorrow, it was a good one to use!

'It would protect them from grasping women, who think they've hit the jackpot,' he said grimly.

'You know nothing about my sister! I hope all Italian men aren't as intransigent as you,' she said scathingly. 'You're blind and prejudiced.' She stood with dignity, her stomach churning. 'You'd better put the cost of the meal on my bill. I'd hate you to think *I* was a grasping woman.'

Max leaned back in his chair, his eyes calculating, and his face stony.

'Tell her it was a very good try,' he said tightly.

Lucy's brow furrowed, not understanding, and ploughed on with the speech she'd been quickly composing in her head.

'You disappoint me. I can see where your sympathies lie and I have no intention of arguing with you any further. Your views are quite wrong, not that it matters.

Now I see what Selina and Renzo are up against and I
intend to do everything I can to help them!'

Thrusting back her chair, she walked away across the
terrace, her head held high, her fists clenched in anger.
Inside was a hollowing misery. The one thing that had
promised to make this journey pleasant, an illogical but
delightful meeting with an attentive and handsome man,
had proved to be a mistake. He was flawed. Sadly she
adjusted to the fact that no man was likely to meet her
high standards.

Once inside the hotel, she ran, as if that would put a
greater distance between her and her disappointment. A
little out of breath from bounding up the stairs, she
rapped lightly on the bedroom door, then more loudly.
There was no answer. A little worried, she called Selina's
name and, when she shook the ill-fitting door, noticed
that the bolt had been drawn across the top. Fear para-
lysed her for a moment, making her stomach lurch.
Maybe Selina had done something really stupid! She'd
been in an awful state. Had she taken something to help
her sleep and blot out her troubles?

Just as she was about to run for help, she noticed that
the door to the adjoining room was open. She hurried
into it, tiptoeing past the cot containing a sleeping baby,
and through the open shutters, remembering that there
was only a low wooden rail between the terraces.

Lucy swung her legs over and strode quickly to her
open door. Somewhere below the terrace, a launch roared
off, startling her. Automatically she turned to see it disappearing towards the distant shore, a high, rolling stern
wave indicating its rapid acceleration. Only dimly did
she register the backward look of a dark-haired man at
the wheel.

Then she was stepping into her room and the shock brought her to a stunned halt.

It was in chaos: drawers upside-down on the bed, her favourite shampoo bottle smashed at her feet, torn pages of the newspaper she'd bought crumpled up as though someone had been using them as missiles. Her feet crunched on to scattered coins. Frantically she searched for her bag and found only her passport. Unable to believe it, she searched every inch of the room, knowing that her passport had been in her bag, and if it was lying around then...

She clutched the side of the wardrobe weakly. Her bag had gone and everything else in it. She was penniless! All the money for Selina, her English money, flight ticket, family photos... With a sob, Lucy realised that she'd lost the only photograph in existence of her father.

'Devils!' she whispered, hurt beyond belief.

Her gaze moved mistily to the cavernous emptiness of the vast wardrobe. They'd taken her clothes. Her few items of clothing. A bedside light had been knocked over and lay on the floor, still switched on, casting strange shadows across the shiny parquet. She slowly picked up the rug which had slid under someone's hasty feet and was crawling up the wall. Mechanically she began to make a methodical inventory before she contacted the hotel management.

The coverlet was missing off the bed. Her shoes had been taken. A shaky dash to the bathroom had her staggering against the door-jamb in disbelief. The thief had taken the few personal items she'd placed there: deodorant, flannel, toothbrush and toothpaste, together with her ribbons, brush and comb. The pettiness of it all!

She closed her eyes, willing it to be a hallucination. But when she opened them again she saw it wasn't and for a moment misery overtook her. What on earth was she to do? Never in her life had she ever imagined that anyone could be so evil. It wasn't as if anything was of value: who would be interested in her few dated clothes, the cheap accessories, her underwear?

Lucy whitened and reached out for the bed, sitting down with a thump. Only a madman or a pervert would have done this—and she'd just realised that Selina was also missing! Nameless horrors filled her brain: of Selina's lovely body, abused, battered. Selina's fears had been justified. Massimo Mazzardi had arranged her disappearance. She reached for the telephone with shaking hands.

CHAPTER FOUR

THEN LUCY spotted the note. Instantly she recognised Selina's handwriting. It was a moment before her eyes focused, and she had to re-read the note several times till she could make sense of it. Even then, her mind seemed unable to comprehend what had happened.

'I didn't tell you everything,' ran the note. 'Renzo and I are more desperate than I said. Wait for my call. In the meantime, don't do anything, don't go to the police or inform the manager and don't see Mazzardi yet. Stay put, or I'll end up in jail. Trust me. Selina.'

Trust her? She stared ahead with sightless eyes. Then she rose, tore up the note and flushed it away. Slowly and deliberately she began to tidy up, using the activity as a means of keeping her from imagining what had caused such desperation, and how she was going to cope without anything but the clothes she stood up in. But with every move she made, the enormity of her situation was driven home more deeply.

Tidier, the room looked barer. Finally she had done all she could and she stood helplessly looking around, all her possessions reduced to the clothes she wore: briefs, a bra, a blouse and skirt and a pair of shoes.

Anger, directed towards her half-sister, welled up inside her. How *could* she? Lucy's furious striding took her out on to the terrace, where the soft night did nothing to alleviate her distress. Why was Selina so impulsive? She'd have her work cut out now, explaining the elopement to the intimidating Mazzardi. It had been bad enough when she was grilled by Max, and he'd liked her to start with! She didn't know how long she stayed out there, upset at the way her love of the world had changed to cynicism. When the telephone rang, and she dashed inside, she discovered that her skin was like ice and so she curled up under the blanket before answering it.

'Thank heaven you're there!' cried Selina's voice.

'Now listen——' began Lucy.

'No, you must! Couldn't explain in the note—too rushed, too dangerous. No time to sneak my things away—had to take yours.'

'Selina——'

'*Please.* You've got to gain us some time before Mazzardi sends out his bloodhounds. Our only hope is to get out of the country. Darling, I swear this is the last thing I'll ever ask you to do, but please, please, go to the island, take my place! Stay in my room, pretend you're ill.'

'What?' cried Lucy, aghast. 'They'll know immediately——'

'Not if you keep the shutters closed and the room dark—you can do it, you must do it! Up to the house, then in the small yellow door round the corner. My room's at the top of the stairs in the attic. It's a dump.'

'But——'

'Listen: Renzo often escapes for a few days, but if they think I've gone too... Oh, Lucy, you don't know how frightened I am! Renzo had to take some money from the safe in Mazzardi's office because Massimo kept him penniless. The way that awful man thinks about me, I'm bound to be blamed. We have to lie low. Forgive me, but we're both terrified of Mazzardi!'

'How much money is involved?' she asked, her mouth dry.

'Thousands. Stall for time. Save me!'

The phone went dead. The receiver fell from Lucy's lifeless hand.

Her one thought was for her sister—and everyone at home. If Lionel ever heard of this, he'd probably have a heart attack at the thought of the child of his middle years, his golden, bubbly, adored Selina, mixed up in theft. Lucy groaned. Whether she wanted to or not, she'd have to go, even if it was only to find a change of clothes. She knelt down and scrabbled for the few scattered coins, counting them quickly. Eleven hundred *lire*. Would that be enough for the boat trip?

She stumbled downstairs and along the weakly lit path to the small jetty.

'Mazzardi,' she said, pushing the coins across the counter. 'The island.'

'*Semplice.*'

'Pardon?' she asked, in agitation.

'No return.' The man, evidently used to confused tourists, scribbled a figure on paper.

Her mind woolly, it was a moment before she grasped that she only had enough cash to buy a single ticket: it would cost double to get a return. She bit her lip, then nodded to the man. Selina would have some cash lying around. She had to. Otherwise, how could she ever get off the island?

Lucy was snatched from sleep by the sound of someone singing loudly in her ear. Pushing her long hair away from her face, she sat bolt upright, her soft hazel eyes searching for the source and discovered to her annoyance that the noise was coming from a small black radio alarm beside the bed. Nervous that it would wake the household and bring people up to her room, she peered at it, looking for the button to turn it off.

'Darn it!' she muttered, finding that the instructions were in Italian.

The tenor's voice echoed richly around the small bare room. Lucy decided to press every button she could see, but the tragic love song still poured forth.

With a defeated groan, she slumped back on the pillows and stuffed them over her head, still reeling from the sudden awakening. Nothing went right for her in this country! Trust Selina to buy a complicated, expensive alarm which looked as if it did everything except turn off.

It had always been difficult to wake Selina each morning. She was a night owl and needed a good shake and a lot of nagging before she would leave her warm nest!

She glanced at the clock. Seven-fifteen. If it hadn't been for the fact that England was operating at an hour behind Italy, she would have woken naturally by this time. She wondered how often Selina had been late for work here before she invested in the alarm. For a brief moment, she felt a twinge of sympathy for Mazzardi, waiting in his innocence for the lovely Selina to turn up to work on time. Poor man. Selina as a sister could be infuriating enough; as an employee she must be exasperating.

Lucy frowned. Had he come up here in a rage himself? No—he would surely have sent a servant, one with a good loud voice! She smiled at the thought of a muscular maid, stomping up the stairs intent on getting Selina out of bed.

This morning, it seemed that the alarm had been set for reveille well before an appearance was needed. The tenor sang his heart out, yet no one had been disturbed apparently: no one banged angrily on the walls or thudded on the door. Still, she mused, the room was tucked away from the main part of the house. It was high in the eaves, small and cramped with a minute and antiquated bathroom attached to it. Mazzardi evidently didn't believe in giving his staff decent accommodation! Her nose wrinkled as her eyes toured the room by the faint light that filtered through the broken shutters. It wasn't the kind of place Selina was used to.

Like any space she occupied, it was chaotic, with clothes dropped haphazardly where she'd taken them off, odd shoes kicked anywhere, open drawers spilling underwear on to the floor and pride of place given to a range of messy make-up in front of a tiny mirror. Lucy felt a tug of affectionate exasperation, and her lip quivered as she wondered how on earth she'd get Selina out of trouble before she had to return to England.

Her first move was to do nothing, of course! Today she had to stay in the room: peeling paint, cracked plaster, noisy radio and all. At least they were broadcasting a quiet love song now. It was rather romantic. She'd leave it on.

Perhaps for a few moments she could open the shutters and let in the sun—that would cheer her up. If she heard anyone coming along to find out why Selina hadn't turned up for work, she could always slam them shut and huddle under the bedclothes pathetically.

As she threw back the covers and made her way to the window, the glorious slide of Selina's black satin nightdress on her skin felt unfamiliar and utterly decadent. She unlocked the small attic window and threw open the shutters to wonderful warm sunshine and blue skies. For a moment she let the sun soak into her face and then leaned out precariously and looked down-wards. Below were the tops of tall palm trees set in beds of exotic plants. Close by on the sunny patio was a large group of people sitting casually at small tables eating breakfast. From her high position at the top of the *palazzo*, it was as if she had a bird's eye view of them—just the tops of their heads, shoulders and an occasional arm as it stretched out to a pile of croissants.

Lucy's empty stomach groaned at the sight of the food, and a brief flash of irritation passed through her mind. It might be an idea to get Selina married off and let someone else cope with her! Then good-natured af-fection and concern surfaced again. A few hunger pangs were nothing to living under the threat of prison, or the distress caused when your fiancé's family wouldn't accept you.

Directly beneath, an elegant dark-clad figure moved as if to rise, and she pulled in her head hurriedly in case he looked up.

How boring it was going to be! There was nothing to do—no books to read, of course—only the room to be tidied. Well, she could start that. The mess was too ap-palling to put up with. It might be an idea to sort out some clothes to wear, ones which would make a suitable impression on Mazzardi. Lucy's mouth formed into a wry smile. Judging by the kind of clothes Selina nor-mally wore, and the garish-coloured garments on the floor, that wasn't very likely, but she couldn't wear her own things. Hindered by the lack of light when she had toiled up the steep servants' staircase, she'd clutched at the walls and transferred their dirt to her good blouse and skirt. They were far too grubby to pass muster.

An authoritative knock on the door brought her heart to her mouth. They'd come for her already—or at least, they'd come for Selina. Lucy flew to close the shutters and leapt into bed, pulling the blankets up around her face and head as an operatic chorus replaced the gentle ballad and noise rocked around the room. She dared not move! Then she remembered. She was safe. The door was firmly bolted.

'Selina!'

Lucy shrank at the angry yell trying to make itself heard. Mazzardi had sent a henchman! The handle of the door turned and she watched in fascinated horror. The room wasn't dark enough for her to escape detection; Selina must have known that, rot her! Lucy set her teeth. She'd have to pretend the room was empty. If she just stayed there, saying nothing, the henchman would have to go away eventually.

Drat that radio! Now she dared not turn it off!

'Selina!'

The man outside uttered a stream of Italian, then there was a pause. 'Open up!'

With the operatic crescendo in the background, it was difficult to hear the muffled voice clearly. Rigoletto's *Verdi* flooded her brain, so that she couldn't think clearly.

'Turn that damn thing off! Let me in!'

Why didn't he give up? Then she realised her stupidity. Automatic radios might be able to turn themselves on and off in empty rooms, but they couldn't bolt doors from the inside. Of course he knew she was in there. Panic-stricken, she gave up and silenced the radio by removing the plug from the socket.

'What was that? I didn't hear you,' she called, trying to mimic Selina's voice.

The man's harsh voice dropped to a menacing snarl. 'Open the door or I'll break it down!'

'I'm not dressed!' she stalled.

'Let me in!'

'What for?'

'You know what for!'

Lucy shook at the low, hoarse sexual threat. In her—Selina's—nightie, she was terribly vulnerable. The man had obviously been led on at some stage and had come to collect! It could be that boatman who had mauled her sister! She plucked at the blankets with trembling fingers, frantically casting around for something to defend herself. There was only one thing in the room of any weight: the radio. In awe of her own intentions, she threw back the blanket and picked up the radio, then hurried hopefully to the window. The terrace below was disappointingly empty. If she screamed, no one would hear. She had to defend herself.

Her heart leapt as the door suddenly shuddered under the impact of a massive body, the wood around the ancient hinges splitting with a terrifying crack. She clenched her teeth and summoned up all her courage, tiptoeing to stand behind the door, the radio poised above her head. The man was like a rampaging bull and she was virtually defenceless. She'd have to hit him the moment he broke in, or she'd have no chance at all. She was fed up with men who wanted to attack her sister. This one would get what he deserved.

With an almighty crash that must have echoed around the whole house, the door caved in under the weight of a man of immense strength. Lucy saw a dark head, a flash of white shirt and then broad, black-suited shoulders hurtled past her with the momentum of the charge. All this she saw in a split second, noting that he'd charged with his right shoulder and that his back was therefore to her.

Before he could turn and take evasive action, she brought the radio hard down on to the back of his head. The man crumpled like a broken puppet to the floor.

From the moment he'd begun to fall, she'd squeezed her eyes together tightly, horrified at the results of her action. She didn't want to look: if she did, she'd feel sorry for him. With an intake of breath, she struggled with her conscience, her eyes opening a mere crack to squint down. There was blood on the back of his skull, trickling through the thick black curls...

She froze. They were like... Reluctant to move her eyes to the man's face, she swallowed, and slowly, hesitantly, her gaze crawled over his neatly shaped ear and the beginning of his jawline. That was all she could see. The rest of his face had become buried in the folds of one of Selina's skirts.

Then he stirred with a groan and his whole body tensed with pain. Lucy took a step back, waving the damaged radio defensively, and then flung it on to the bed in disgust at herself. The man was injured and she had to do something.

Whirling around, she ran into the tiny bathroom and soaked a towel in cold water. When she returned, he was sitting up, facing her, feeling the back of his head cautiously.

She felt her legs turn to stone. She stood in the bathroom doorway, rooted to the spot, a terrible churning sensation in her stomach.

The man's thick fringe of lashes lifted with agonising slowness; to her bare feet, up the clinging narrow satin with the long slit to the upper thigh, over her gently swelling stomach, to her pearly, half-exposed breasts, rising and falling heavily with horror, and then, finally, to her face.

His eyes widened, then the heavy lids dropped and he shut his eyes tightly, shaking his head as he did so and cursing at the pain. Lucy just stood there, immobile, water from the towel dripping gently on to the tiled floor.

She was fixed by his accusing eyes again.

'Lucinda?' whispered Max, as if he couldn't believe what he was seeing.

Something cold trickled around her toes, and in a dream she looked down, seeing the water. She also saw her state of undress. Her mind in total confusion, she whirled around and yanked at the sheet, tugging almost hysterically when it failed to be extricated easily and gasping with relief when she could wrap it around herself at last and gain some appearance of decency. All the time, he had been watching her as if he couldn't believe his eyes.

Max looked stunned. She might have killed him! 'Here,' she said in a breathy, choking voice, kneeling down. 'Let me see to your head.'

'Someone hit me,' he said slowly, his lips finding difficulty in mouthing the words.

'Yes.' Lucy was gently cleaning the wound, trying not to let her heart lurch at his helplessness. His thick black lashes lay on his cheeks and his skin was drawn taut in pain, emphasising the aristocratic angle of his jaw, the haughty line of his nose and sheer purity of his cheekbone. Freshly shaven, satin-smooth and deeply tanned, the hollow of his cheek demanded her touch and made her fingers tingle. He looked like a little boy, with his tumbled curls and confused expression, and the sight wrenched at her within, her heart somersaulting in an inexplicable affection.

She tried to master the storm of feeling that made her head spin. 'It's not too bad, I've seen worse. Heads bleed a lot.'

Tentatively, her fingers explored his scalp, the sensation of warm, silky hair apparently trying to curl around her fingers and capture them making her tremble. He groaned and grabbed her around the waist for support when her forefinger gently traced the outline of the bump on his head. They were close. Their very warmth was mingling. His breath was making the exposed skin beneath her collarbone incredibly sensitive.

In her innocence and anxiety, she had knelt at his side, supporting his left shoulder with one hand; the other now slipping uncertainly down the nape of his neck. It was warm and smooth, she thought incoherently, her fingers lingering.

Pain seemed to be making his breath hotter, faster, more rasping. It seared her skin now and Lucy found that she was breathing in unison with him. Their faces were inches apart; she fixed her tensed gaze on the intricate folds of his ear and the way his black hair had been disciplined into a neat shape in front of it. She knew what he was staring at. Her breasts rose with the tiny shuddering breath she gave at the thought. He would be looking down with his sultry, hot eyes, her swelling flesh beneath the thin sheet almost touching his chest.

His shudder echoed hers and Lucy quivered at his long, ragged exhalation. He was as confused as she. Neither of them thought it odd that his hands should slide slowly in an exploration, enjoying the feel of the wickedly smooth, inviting satin as the sheet moved under his touch. His long fingers trailed over her hips, ran upwards, tantalisingly short of her breasts, and then downwards again, both of them revelling in the sensory experience. Lucy's head tipped right back in a desperate attempt to conquer the consuming desire that coursed fiercely through every part of her body and threatened to vanquish all her inhibitions.

'Lucinda!' he whispered, in a barely audible voice.

Her head slowly returned and her eyes rested on him, the intensity of his magnetism compelling her to meet his heavy-lidded gaze. The air was charged with sexual tension: elemental, primitive, heedless of rules and morals. Lucy yearned to dig her fingers in his shoulders and demand that he kiss her, and the knowledge stunned her.

His eyes seemed to be flowing into her, black and inviting. The heat of his hands burned now into her slender back, and she could feel the bones of her spine beneath them. She was speechless with the shock of desire, aware that her lids were half closing, her nostrils flaring, and helpless to prevent even her lips from parting. Mesmerised, she saw the slight curl and parting of his lips; a movement so strongly sensual that every nerve in her body sprang alive.

She swayed on her knees beside him, an unconscious invitation of her supple body and one to which he responded immediately. Warning bells sounded in Lucy's head, but her movements were so reluctant and languorous that his hands were gently unwrapping the sheet and cupping her satin-cased breasts wonderingly before she could stop him.

The shock ran through her like a rippling wave. Her slumbering, smouldering eyes widened and her head cleared. Deftly she slipped away, shaking from her wanton behaviour, bewildered that she could have behaved so badly. Awkwardly she stumbled to her feet, pulling the sheet protectively around herself again, appalled that she had so little control where he was concerned.

'What——?' Max's black brows met. 'What the hell——'

He stopped, a look of anguish on his face, but somehow she knew that it wasn't connected with his injury. And her instincts were confirmed when he looked at her as if he didn't want to credit his own thoughts.

The situation cleared for her too. She took a few steps back. A man had tried to force his way into Selina's room. A man with vile intentions. Maybe the sex-crazed boatman who had assaulted Selina, she had thought. Max was that man. He was handsome enough to think he was irresistible, experienced enough—by what she had just been subjected to—to recognise Selina's sex appeal, and... Lucy shut her eyes in distress. He was a boatman. That smart boat could well be owned by Mazzardi.

When Max had been rejected by Selina, he'd been so frustrated that he'd decided to make do with second-best! She kicked herself for being so susceptible to such an out-and-out sex-mad monster, and her whole body began to quiver with fury.

'You beast!' she hurled through her teeth. 'You disgusting, evil brute! You deserve that crack on the head. I only wish I'd laid you out completely. I hope it hurts for days! Now get out of here before I yell for help.'

He was on his knees and groggily standing in seconds. 'You have a nerve!' he breathed in wonder. '*You* are throwing *me* out?'

'Darn right I am!' she yelled, her hair a mass of angry red. 'You arrogant swine!'

'Well,' he growled, raking her up and down with carnal eyes. 'You've changed since last night. There's a marked difference in your clothes and manner. Where has the demure, threadbare little miss gone?'

'I might seem meek on the outside to some people,' she seethed, her eyes glittering, 'but inside I can be as tough as anyone when necessary.'

'So much for the *madonna*,' he said with a cynical twist to his mouth. 'I thought you were too good to be true.' He had retreated behind an implacable mask. Even his eyes were shuttered, betraying no emotion. Only his tensed muscles betrayed the fact that he was checking a volcanic temper. 'It seems, when it comes down to it, you can be as much of a bitch and a slut as your sister.'

'How dare you?' Lucy gasped in outrage, secretly worrying just what Selina had got up to with this man, to deserve that insult. Perhaps her sister's response had been innocent, like hers just now. She'd been confused, muddled, she'd thought he was hurt and wanted... Her face flamed. She knew very well what she had wanted.

He drew in a deep breath. 'At least Selina is honest about sex. Whereas you... Hell, I ought to slap your deceiving, innocent face!' he hissed. 'She's obvious. You get under a man's skin in a way that's far more seductive and erotic.'

He took a few steps towards her, and she backed away till she felt the wall behind her. She was cornered. Max came on, nothing in his expression at all, and that terrified her. He was going to take his revenge, and she was in no doubt what that would be. Sexuality poured from his body in the way he stalked towards her. It reached out and clutched her with its heat, and Lucy felt its pagan pull. She was unable to prevent her lashes from dropping slightly, and knew her eyes glowed and liquefied.

Max's eyes smouldered darkly in response. Her lips opened and she tried to force out a protest, to deny him,

but a cruel anger had flickered over his features and he
had covered the short distance between them with an
impatient stride; his arms had crushed her body and her
head had been snapped back by the sudden assault of
his ruthless, bruising lips grinding into hers.

There was a hard desperation in the kiss, a cruelty
that made her want to weep. Petrified at his violence,
she tried to struggle, but he was far too strong, his hands
exploring her body with crude insult as if she were merely
a sex object, to be used for his immediate satisfaction
and then discarded.

'You bastard!' she spat, when his hard, grinding
mouth drew away. Lucy had never used such a word
before. He was the first man she'd met who had really
deserved it.

In a contemptuous movement he released her, his bulk
and vicious temper still intimidating her, blistering scorn
pouring from his body. The bright diamonds of her eyes
flashed a message back: she despised him and his kind.

'Touch me again and I'll make you rue the day you
set eyes on me,' she threatened in a low voice.

He laughed nastily and placed his big hands on the
wall, either side of her head. Lucy clenched her fists,
ready. Then his face soured.

'Too late, madonna. I do already. Just tell me what
you're doing here,' he said grimly.

'What *I'm* doing here?' she asked. 'What about you?'

'I have a reason,' he growled.

'So I discovered,' she said scathingly.

'Stop evading the question.' He had control of himself
again and the husky voice slid silkily, hiding all but a
tinge of steel. 'We have all the time we want,' he said
in a softly menacing tone. 'I can make you do anything

I wish. I can certainly think of a satisfying way to persuade you to talk.'

'What do you want to know?' she gulped.

'What you're doing here,' he repeated, the hunch of
his shoulders reminding her of his suppressed power.

'Disappointed that Selina isn't here?' she threw at him.

'Yes. Naturally.'

That truth sliced through her like a knife. Her sister
could have been deflowered by this rake! Thank heavens
they'd changed places! Selina's beauty would have been
too much for him to resist.

'She's out.' She intended to make his search for Selina
as difficult as possible. Raw hatred of him seared into
every bone in her body.

'I can see that!' he snarled. 'Where?'

'I don't know.' She flung up her chin defiantly, and
almost as quickly it was grasped between a hurting finger
and thumb.

'I don't advise you to play cat and mouse with me,'
he grated through clenched teeth. 'You are the bait, after
all.'

The look he gave her made her shiver. There was a
definite sexual threat in that, and the way his voice grew
even huskier told her that he could still be physically
aroused. Heat curled down to her toes at the sensual
softening of his mouth. She wriggled under his scrutiny.

'Utterly without morals, the two of you,' he sneered.
'I want to know where she is.'

'I told you. I don't know. Are you intending to foist
your unwelcome attentions on her again?'

He stopped in surprise. 'What?'

'You heard.'

'I am expecting her to turn up for her job on time for
once.'

'Oh, yes?' she said in disbelief. 'Why should her punctuality interest you?'

'You know she works for me.'

'Don't be stupid, she...' Lucy paused, examining the perfectly tailored charcoal suit, the dazzling white shirt, the sober black tie, slightly askew. She saw for the first time the glitter of gold on his cuffs, and as he folded his arms across his rapidly rising chest she also saw a massive gold watch on his wrist. 'She told me she was a guide here. You're... you're a boatman, Max the boatman!'

Her voice died away and she looked at him questioningly, puzzled by it all.

He gave her a false smile and applauded. 'Terribly good. Superlative, in fact. I congratulate you. How lucky Selina is to have such a deceptive sister.'

'I don't know what you're talking about!' she snapped. 'What are you doing, wearing that suit? Were you trying to impress Selina?'

'Impress her?' he frowned. 'These are my normal working clothes.'

'Really? Then what were you doing earlier in those ragged shorts? And you didn't look like a tailor's dummy when we had dinner!' She was pleased that he winced at the insult. In fact, no man had ever looked less like a dummy. Now he had straightened his tie, he looked immaculate, businesslike, unnervingly virile and utterly devastating.

'You don't repair boat engines in suits. As for dinner, well, I thought you might be intimidated if I turned up in a suit.'

'Oh, for heaven's sake,' she said in irritation, 'I've seen men in suits before.'

'And out of them, no doubt. What about you?' he continued bitterly. 'You wore prim clothes, an innocent look and talked of caring for the elderly. We played our parts well, didn't we?'

She passed a shaking hand over her face, trying to make sense of the situation.

'Get dressed,' he ordered.

'Get out,' she countered stubbornly.

He rocked on his heels, as if he was master of all he surveyed. 'Either dress now, or I will do it for you. Choose.'

She took one look at his stony, cold face and felt the fear trickle inside her. 'All right,' she said firmly. 'I will.'

She waited for him to leave, but he stood there, rock still and glaring balefully.

'I can't dress with you watching,' she whispered, her throat dry.

'I'm not leaving. I'm keeping you in my sight.'

She licked her lips under his merciless eyes. An unpleasant icy smile spread slowly over his face. He reached for a pair of delicate lace briefs on the floor and began to move towards her, a look of intent on his face.

'No, I'll do it! Don't touch me, I don't want you to touch me!' She shuddered.

The briefs were thrown dismissively towards her. She eyed them uncertainly, wishing Selina hadn't such sensual taste, then a slight movement of Max's leg muscles threw her into activity.

Totally humiliated, she dressed with as much decency as she was able, using the sheet for protection from his lustful gaze, knowing that her body was no longer its usual pallor but had been suffused with colour. All she could find within arm's reach was either a skimpy top and a pair of incredibly brief shorts, or a halter-necked dress in a glaring red. Not daring to push past him and risk his wandering hands again, she angrily pulled on

the dress, only to find that it was one of Selina's more
suggestive purchases. In dismay she tried to adjust the
neckline so that it didn't look as if she had deliberately
pushed her breasts up in order to be provocative.

'Leave it.'

Lucy was startled at the thickened tone and miserably
realised that the clinging dress was provoking him
whether she liked it or not. Blindly she bent to push her
feet into her own shoes, mercifully this side of the bed,
innocently unaware that her thick lustrous hair was tumbling forwards in a shimmering curtain and drawing attention to her cleavage. Max gave a sharp intake of breath
and yanked her upright.

'You calculating bitch!' he whispered. 'I've a good
mind to give you what you're asking for!'

She was in no doubt as to what he meant, but she was
furious that he was one of those men who imagined every
woman was eager and throbbing with desire for them.
She was even angrier with herself for not thinking about
the way she was dressed, but she'd never needed to
before.

'Your touch sickens me,' she said coldly. 'I'm quite
innocent of any seduction.'

He gave a cynical laugh. 'Downstairs.'

'I haven't done my hair yet.' She lifted her arms, pre-
paratory to tucking it back to receive its customary neat
ribbon.

Max's lips whitened and he roughly dragged her arms
down. 'Give up,' he grated. 'I don't go with whores.'

Lucy wriggled in his grasp vigorously, his fingers
closing like a steel trap around her slender wrists.

'You swine!' she half sobbed. 'You filthy, degraded
swine! You don't even know a decent woman when you
see one.'

'*No!*' he roared, unleashing his suppressed anger at last. 'You're damn right I don't. I've learnt that, at least!' He pulled her to him, his eyes glittering, his teeth bared in a snarl. 'I thought I did and I was mistaken. Now, Jezebel, keep your hair loose. It suits the tarty dress better and helps me to remember what you are.'

He pushed her away and dusted off his hands as if he had soiled them. She was almost beside herself with anger. She planted her hands on her hips and took in a deep breath.

'I've got one or two things to say to you,' she seethed, 'and you'd better listen to me carefully. And then I intend taking you to the police and charging you with assault— maybe for attempted rape, too!'

The lines around Max's mouth told of his disdain. But she sensed that it was a little assumed. Behind the façade, she thought she saw a grudging admiration. Feeling a little more in control of the situation, she fixed him with her famous icy stare.

Ignoring it, he stepped on to the remnants of the splintered door and gestured abruptly for her to leave the room.

She thought rapidly. Anywhere was better than here. And if Mazzardi himself got to hear that Selina was missing from the attic room, she could still hold him at bay too, and gain Selina and Renzo a little more time to flee from this awful house.

To her surprise, instead of directing her to the back stairs, he took her to wider, carpeted steps which spiralled down till they were at the end of a long gallery hung with portraits. In cold silence she walked ahead, conscious that his hot breath was fanning her shoulders.

After passing huge ornate wooden doors leading, presumably to various bedrooms, they came out on to a broad landing at the top of a beautiful double flight of stairs covered in a thick peach carpet. Her suspicions grew. He was remarkably confident in using the main stairway. This was no boatman, despite the fact that he had been mending the engine. He was something higher up in the hierarchy, probably one of Mazzardi's henchmen, one of his 'hit men'. That would explain all the muscles.

She could have kicked herself, telling him so much about Selina during dinner. He must have been laughing at her all the time, egging her on to give out more information. It wouldn't surprise her in the least to learn that he had acted as some kind of spy, and all his initial charm and potent allure had been calculated to attract a stupid, gullible English girl. Her hatred of him intensified. It was rare that she allowed herself to let anyone see her vulnerability, always preferring to stay in control of situations. Max had swept her off her feet and cruelly exposed her weakness for romance. For that, she'd never forgive him.

'Are you taking me to Mazzardi?' she asked sullenly.

He threw her an exasperated look. 'In there.'

Lucy crossed the huge marble-floored hall with its dazzling chandelier, sparkling in the sunlight streaming through the enormous windows. Bright patterns danced on the floor where she walked, making her blink.

'Does he speak English?' she demanded.

Max pushed her inside, slammed the door and leaned against it heavily. 'Don't push me any further. Know when to stop. You've already been closer to physical harm than any woman I've ever known. Don't shame me and chance a violent reaction by making me lose control again. It's over. We're going to have a serious discussion.'

'I think I'd rather wait till you've taken hold of yourself,' she said firmly, inwardly quaking at his thunderous face. It would be better to talk to the owner; he'd be more civilised. 'Where's Massimo Mazzardi? I want to speak to him.'

'Damn you!' roared Max. 'You know perfectly well that I'm Mazzardi! Drop the innocence, I've had enough of it!'

CHAPTER FIVE

LUCY'S eyes widened. 'That's ridiculous! You——' Her voice died, choked by the lump of fear in her throat. For several seconds she scanned his face, seeing there the hauteur, the arrogance and the cruelty that Selina had told her about. The muscles in her stomach clenched and she felt suddenly weak. Everything fitted; everything made sense. Oh, lord, she thought weakly, he spoke the truth—and he knew everything!

'You did know,' he insisted. 'You and Selina planned it all. I must admit, she chose well. Who would imagine that a flustered, naïve and shabbily dressed woman could be so devious? You played me for a sucker,' he snarled, 'and I fell for it like an idiot. How could I be so gullible? I've survived the traps of countless scheming women, only to drop into the least expected one. Such sweetness and light! A noble, heroic, admirable woman, working her fingers to the bone——'

'Stop it!' she cried in despair, shaking her head in denial. 'I didn't know who you were, I thought you were just a poor boatman——'

'With a boat like that?' he scorned. 'Do you really expect me to believe that out of all those launches you chose mine by coincidence? That all those lies you told me——' To her distress, he began to mimic her voice in a sickly, mincing tone. 'Oh, Max, I have a poor arthritic mother! My job is incredibly rewarding! I'm not keen on brash young men; I can't shimmer——'

'Don't!' Lucy put her hands over her ears, but they were dragged down and Max Mazzardi was close, his shoulders angrily squared, his face implacable in its hatred.

'Oh, yes,' he whispered in soft malevolence. 'It all sounds stupid now, doesn't it? But I was ready to believe it, almost desperate to believe. I wanted to think that I'd met a woman who wasn't a hard-bitten, grasping, devious bitch for a change.' He laughed harshly, the bitter sound making Lucy cringe. 'Instead,' he muttered almost to himself, 'I'd met my match. A cruel witch inside an angel.'

Tears started in her eyes. 'You're wrong, Max,' she whispered. 'I'm innocent of all you accuse me. And you lied: you gave me a false name. You're called Massimo.'

'I told no lies,' he rasped. 'Max is the name my friends use. Not, you notice, my family, or employees I don't trust. My close friends. Italians have a habit of using pet names.'

Pet! She almost laughed. He was like no pet she'd ever known. More like a very dangerous wounded animal. She was well aware that Italian men were very proud, and he seemed to think that she'd tried to scheme and divert him away from Selina. She groaned inwardly. This was Massimo, then, the man her sister had said was callous and cruel. That was painfully obvious. No wonder he'd frightened Selina and Renzo. His sinister, underhand behaviour and calculating mind would unnerve most people.

'I can't stop you thinking whatever you please,' she said quietly. 'All I can say is that when I arrived in Stresa I was worried about Selina. I did make a mistake in choosing your boat—and what a mistake! I wish with all my heart that I'd searched for the proper boatmen instead of blindly stepping into your wretched launch!'

'Don't start that again! To think I confided in you some of my innermost, secret feelings,' he seethed. 'You made an absolute fool of me and I will never forget that!'

No. He was too macho, too wrapped up in his own sense of importance. All she could do was to insist quietly. 'Everything I said was true. Check if you like. You misjudge me,' she said doggedly.

For a long moment he frowned at her, attempting to intimidate her with his piercing gaze, but she knew she was in the right and never faltered. Eventually it was he who dropped his eyes. Relief flooded through Lucy. Maybe he now believed her. With that relief came exhaustion. Strong as she was, the physical and emotional toll of the past couple of days had been too much for anyone to bear. She felt her knees buckle and clutched at the desk.

'What's the matter with you now? Playing for sympathy?' he asked coldly.

In answer, her stomach rumbled and rolled. 'Excuse me,' she muttered, embarrassed. 'I haven't eaten for a long, long time.' Pride prevented her from asking him for anything. Though without any money... Her eyes filled with tears and she sat down quickly in a chair, wishing her body didn't tremble so badly.

Max Mazzardi barked instructions down a telephone. There was a silence apart from the sound of his feet as he paced up and down on the gold marble floor, and occasionally he came close enough for her to hear his heavy breathing. He was still ferociously angry, and it was an anger far greater than Lucy thought was warranted. His pride must be of the utmost importance to him.

Wearily she lifted her head. They were in a study, the walls lined with enormous old books, some bound in gold-tooled leather, all carefully chained. Above, the ceiling soared like a cupola, holding Lucy's attention with its detailed paintings of romping gods and goddesses.

The back of her neck prickled and she whipped her head around to find Max studying her thoughtfully. His arrogant chin lifted, and as hers did too he arched a sardonic brow.

'Calculating my market value?' he murmured sarcastically, a supercilious lift to his brows.

His remark wasn't worthy of an answer. Instead she scanned the rest of the room with its comfortable antique furniture and admired its effortless, elegant grace.

A man, dressed in an open-necked T-shirt, black jeans and trainers, brought in a tray loaded with coffee, hot croissants, honey, cake and fruit. With a pleasant word to Mazzardi, he politely placed a low table in front of Lucy, gave her an easy grin and left.

'Eat,' said Max. 'Then you talk. And you'll tell me everything.' He sat down opposite her, a menacing, threatening figure. 'But while you eat, consider this.' She looked up, alerted by the sudden triumphant ring to his voice. He was smiling with a twisted mouth, his face imperious and full of contempt. 'From this moment on you must consider yourself my hostage,' he said softly. 'My prisoner. Until Selina returns, I intend to hold you here, on this island. My prisoner, Lucinda! And if you think I've been hard on you so far, then you have an unpleasant surprise coming, because I've hardly begun the punishment you deserve. It will be the punishment for a deceiver, a potential whore, and an accessory to grand larceny. I swear this: I will make you suffer for what the two of you have done to me and my family!'

Lucy was beginning to get the measure of Max Mazzardi. She ignored his empty threat and made a great play of buttering a croissant and spreading it liberally with honey. In this day and age, people couldn't possibly treat you like a hostage—not without an armed guard, anyway. It would be child's play to get away from the island.

'Did you hear me?' asked Max grimly.

'Oh, yes. But I don't fall for your bullying tactics. You see, Mr Mazzardi, I've been up against your type before.'

'Indeed?' he drawled.

She nodded. 'Mmm. Nasty bureaucrats who regard their tidy rules and red tape as being more important than elderly people who haven't the ability to fight for their own rights. Intimidation I'm used to.'

'You seem to be losing that bewildered, little girl lost attitude remarkably quickly,' he said with soft menace.

'I am, aren't I?' she said thoughtfully. 'It seems that one country is much like another, really. There are good people in them and . . .' she shot him an accusing glare, 'a great deal of evil and misuse of power. Now tell me, why does a wealthy man like you masquerade as a ragged boatman and mend his own engines? Don't you have others to do that for you at your beck and call, or had you mislaid your whip that morning?'

A flicker of amusement twitched at his mouth and was hastily suppressed. 'I need no whip. I control people by sheer force of personality alone. One of my beliefs is that I should be prepared to get my hands dirty sometimes and not spend all day dictating from a desk. Besides, it was a beautiful day and the lake beckoned. I needed freedom from paperwork and the ever-ringing telephone. Even evil bullies like to relax.'

Lucy disregarded the mockery in his eyes and reached for another croissant. 'I'm glad you've recognised your character. It could be the first step towards improving it.'

She was amazed at herself, bandying words with this sophisticated Italian! But all her gentle nature had been outraged by his behaviour, and she was finding within herself that remarkable quality which Lionel referred to as her 'mother hen syndrome'. Whenever any of her charges or her family were threatened or criticised by an outsider, she defended them to the last.

Max was chuckling. 'I'm going to enjoy being your gaoler,' he said in a soft growl, as if her challenge was sexually exciting.

She felt a flash of fear. He'd got the wrong end of the stick about her and might try anything! Her only defence was common-sense talking. Pouring herself a cup of coffee, she glanced up at him. 'You didn't tell me who you were. You could have done. Why didn't you just turn me off the boat?'

He frowned. 'I wish I had,' he said shortly. 'You seemed so damned vulnerable, and I reckoned it was better to play along and not embarrass you.'

'How kind,' she said, not believing a word.

'Yes,' he hissed. 'It was!'

'Were you being kind by flirting with me, too?' she asked lightly, her heart thumping crazily. 'Did you think that was what I expected from you?'

There was no answer. Lucy raised her lashes to see that he was staring helplessly at her, almost defenceless. Then his mouth firmed.

'That's right,' he snapped.

Suddenly she felt like slumping, defeated. So she'd been right. There was no chemistry, only his clever pretence. It must have amused him to see how easy it was for him to turn her head. So much for her wild imagination. Serve her right that her fingers had been burnt and her heart scalded because of her stupid dreaming. That would teach her to have too high an opinion of herself.

'You didn't have to ask me out to dinner,' she whispered. 'Did you think you'd learn more about me? Or had you discovered your bed was empty and you reckoned I was a pushover?'

'I was at a loose end,' he answered without expression.

'That's very cruel,' she said quietly.

'Lucinda——' Max rose abruptly and stalked over to the window. Then he swung around, his face dark. 'We've spent a while answering your questions. You've been very clever, delaying me.'

'I don't understand,' she began.

'Your sister is missing. You must tell me where she is,' he said, barely controlling his impatience. 'It would be better for her and for Renzo if they're brought back here before they do anything stupid.'

'Like getting married, you mean?' she shot.

He blanched, then collected himself together and sat down again, drawing his chair close to her.

'Look,' he said in a reasoning tone, 'they're totally unsuited. The marriage would be a disaster——'

'She said you were a snob,' observed Lucy calmly.

'Damn!' He brought his fist down on the low table, making the crockery jump.

'She also said you had a filthy temper.'

'It's hardly surprising, under the circumstances,' he said. 'I don't know how you can sit there so calmly. I give you one last chance and then I'm calling in the police. I will not let my brother marry a thief.'

Lucy glared. 'Selina's no thief!'

'She took money from my safe,' he said grimly.

'No, it wasn't her!' Now what should she do? Tell him it was his brother?

'All the staff here, with the exception of your sister, have been with my family for years. Nothing has gone missing before. Suddenly my safe is empty and I have lost *lire* worth thousands of pounds sterling.'

'You have no proof it's Selina! Why would she take your money? How could she open your safe?'

'Renzo has a key. No doubt she persuaded him to go along with her scheme. She has already borrowed heavily against her future wages. The shops in Stresa are reeling from her spending sprees. Your sister has a love of money and well you know it.'

It was a pity she couldn't deny that. But she owed loyalty to Selina. Max had to be told the truth.

'It hasn't occurred to you that Renzo could have taken the money? He was only taking his share. It's all your fault, really. How could he survive without any? You kept him penniless, you wanted it all for yourself——'

His mouth twisted. 'Is that what she told you?' he demanded.

'Yes, of course!'

'Renzo took more than his "share", as you call it. The safe is *completely* empty. And why are my grandmother's jewels also missing?' he asked, his face inches away from hers.

She recoiled. 'You're lying...'

'You want to meet my grandmother? To see her distress? To hear how those jewels were destined for my future wife, the next mistress of Isola Mazzardi? You've been fooled by your half-sister. She's used you as she used me and as she is using Renzo to acquire for herself riches beyond her dreams.'

'No, you're wrong,' moaned Lucy. Selina was foolish, but not downright wicked.

His fingers caught her chin and forced her to look into his eyes. 'You look at me. Look well. See my anger. See how insulted I am that I should take into my house a woman who not only endangers the reputation of Isola Mazzardi by the sloppy, lazy manner in which she guided our tours, but whose greedy eyes fell on my impressionable brother and who plotted his downfall. This, I might tell you, was after she tried to get me interested in her.'

'No, please don't,' whispered Lucy. Who could blame Selina for being initially attracted to Max? Without knowing his evil character, he had the kind of raw animal magnetism that would draw any woman!

'Where is she?' he demanded relentlessly.

'I don't know, I honestly don't know!'

'You must have some idea,' he persisted. 'I've had the lake police watching for days. None of my boats are missing. No one answering her description has hired a launch. Renzo vanished from Isola dei Pescatori yesterday evening. From what you told me, your sister was in your room then. You must have had a hand in her escape! Perhaps you were the plain, drably dressed tourist who paid for a pleasure-boat in English money—though the man swore he would have remembered if she had red hair.'

Lucy's eyes widened and then darted away from his, but he'd seen the flash of realisation in them.

'You know something. Tell me!'

She bit her lip, thinking hard, torn between shielding the thoughtless Selina and stopping her from marrying in haste. How ordinary would she look, if she wore plain clothes and no make-up, and drew her hair back simply? Mazzardi's men might well ignore someone so dull-looking if they were looking for a woman as beautiful as Selina.

Only Lucy knew how much of that beauty was an ability her sister had to make the most of herself, after a considerable period in front of the mirror. So that was why her clothes had been taken. Selina had realised what a good disguise they would make! Bitterness curled in Lucy's stomach. Selina had been blatantly calculating when she rang pleading for help. She had wanted a dupe. Even if Lucy hadn't left the coast clear by spending time with Max, encouraged by the supposedly tired Selina, there would have been other opportunities. The scheming little minx! No wonder she'd looked apologetic when Lucy had left.

It hurt Lucy acutely that Selina had been so deceitful.

'Your face tells me everything,' said Max harshly. 'You are beginning to realise you've been fooled by a very clever couple. What kind of woman would leave another to face the music?' he demanded. 'She knew me and my opinion of her. She must also have known how angry I would be when I found out you'd aided and abetted her.'

'I didn't! I was all for coming to the island and persuading you to give them a chance to prove their love, with a long engagement.'

'Really? So what happened to make you change your mind?' he growled. 'I recall you saying that you intended to do everything you could to help Selina. Tell me, why were you in her room?'

She was caught. If she told him how Selina had slipped off with all her possessions while she was having dinner, he would think even worse of her sister than he did at the moment. If Renzo and Selina did eventually marry, they'd be off to a bad start. She had to protect them. She shrugged.

'I see.' He sounded disappointed, and Lucy longed to tell him the truth. Now she understood his anger. However misguided he was in standing in the way of two people in love, she had to admit that their behaviour hadn't been likely to endear him to them. Theft and deception, particularly theft from an elderly lady, was despicable. And all the time Max had been so foul to her in the attic room just now, he'd believed that she was in on the deception. He imagined that she was acting as a willing decoy. No wonder he was bitter!

'It's all lies, isn't it? You're still trying to protect yourself from me. You didn't plan to act the big sister and mediate between Selina and me. Your role was to flutter helplessly and use your angel face to keep my mind off Renzo's disappearance. And this morning, your body was on offer and I was almost lured again. *Dio!* I could have spent days in bed with you! I might have forgotten everything, in the lying tenderness in your eyes. You never were the kind of woman I first believed you to be! This is the real you, isn't it?' He indicated her revealing dress. 'This and the black satin nightdress, the sluttish mess in the room with all your clothes and make-up everywhere, after hunting for the most seductive nightwear you could find—that was you!'

Lucy stared at him miserably, powerless to deny it without him demanding another explanation and perhaps finding out the truth. It didn't matter what he thought of her, it didn't!

Max glowered at her silence. 'So you did know who I was when you agreed to have dinner with me. Your sister had persuaded you to keep me occupied while she stripped my safe and did her disappearing trick! And everything that followed was an act,' he muttered. 'You deliberately set out to seduce me.'

'Don't flatter yourself!' she snapped.

'Oh? Surely you're not going to pretend that all that abandoned tousled hair and the carefully rising breasts was innocent? You can hardly deny that you wanted me, not the way you responded when I touched you.'

'I do deny it,' she breathed.

'Dammit, Lucinda,' he growled. 'I know when a woman is aroused.'

'Don't mistake anger and disgust for arousal,' she shot.

He let go of her chin and leaned back in the chair as if exhausted, pressing a button on the telephone.

'Signore?'

Max turned wearily to the man in the sports shirt and jeans who had entered, and motioned for him to remove the tray.

'Mal di testa forte, Paolo. Mi porti una tisana.'

Lucy didn't understand what he said, but did interpret the way he pressed his hands to his temples.

'Max—I'm awfully sorry I hit you,' she said, miserably. With all that had happened, it had completely slipped her mind that she'd beaten him over the head with the radio!

'Was that assault another attempt to stall for time?' he asked, shutting his eyes and massaging the throbbing pulse spots on either side of his head.

'No,' she denied miserably. 'I thought you were coming to—to rape Selina,' she finished in a low tone.

A jaundiced eye flicked up at her. 'Oh, yes?'

'Yes! With the radio blaring, I couldn't hear who it was, only that there was an aggressive man trying to get in.'

'At seven-thirty in the morning?' he drawled.

'You have specific times for sex?' she asked coldly.

He gave a mocking laugh. 'It seems I haven't,' he murmured, running assessing eyes over her body.

'That's what I thought,' she said angrily. 'Selina's always been bothered by men like you, leering at her. She's always having to fight them off. They treat her as if she was a . . .' She stopped, confused, realising that she wasn't painting a very good picture.

'As if she was a tart?' suggested Max coldly, accepting gratefully the medicinal tisane from Paolo.

Lucy flushed and bridled. 'Men shouldn't think that of a woman without good reason,' she began.

'Exactly.' He stayed her protest with an authoritative hand. 'So you're claiming that you hadn't been told what to do when I came to Selina's room to check up on her?'

'No! How would she know that you'd trail all the way up to her room, anyway? Can you prove that you weren't intending to catch her in bed and take advantage of her?' she accused.

'I can prove your sister is more devious than either of us could imagine. She knew full well that I would be checking up on her when both she and my brother didn't appear for breakfast,' he said in a deadly tone. 'Even before I had my suspicions that she was thinking of eloping with him, she was often late down and someone would go up to get her out of bed. Usually one of the maids,' he added, at Lucy's shocked expression.

As she digested this, struggling with the knowledge that she'd been callously thrown in at the deep end by her sister, Max gave a mirthless laugh.

'In any case, the idea of me clambering up all those stairs for an early-morning rape is ludicrous.' His head lifted arrogantly, an autocratic sneer touching his lips and a soft, triumphant tone to his voice. 'I keep my emotions under control.'

'You could have fooled me,' she muttered.

'There are times,' he said tightly, 'when a person needs a lesson from me.'

'A lesson in how crude men can be?' she countered.

His eyes blazed. 'And I mistakenly likened you to a fragile, shy flower!'

'I will defend my family to the end,' she said quietly.

He studied her for a moment, his face impassive. 'You're loyal, I'll give you that. Well, let's see how far your loyalty goes. Until your sister returns, you must stay here. I intend to get my money's worth from the Parish girls.'

'What do you mean by that?' she asked in horror. She had to return home. Then she remembered. Selina had her handbag containing her money and ticket. Lucy went white.

'You'll damn well do her job. I'll work you till you drop. And more.'

'You can't make me!'

'No. But do you want the police brought in? Normally I don't use my power and position, but this is a special case and I intend to pull every string I can to bend Selina, Renzo...' His eyes caressed her mockingly. '...and you, to my will. I am a very influential man here. The police are likely to believe me. Your sister could be in prison for fifteen years. All her superficial beauty will be gone by then,' he said coldly. 'How do you think she would like it, without a full-length mirror, pretty clothes and make-up? How would she like the plain food, the bare walls——'

'Stop it!' cried Lucy, preventing him from painting his horrible picture. She couldn't bear any more. It was possible that Selina and Renzo hadn't left the country yet. If Mazzardi brought in the police and managed to trace them both, she could be condemning Selina to a ruined future. She might not have taken the money, but she must surely be an accessory after the fact. And it looked as if Max was prepared to do anything in revenge.

Somehow she'd get a telephone message home: sneak into his office if necessary, as Selina had. The stand-in had offered to stay longer if Lucy wanted. She'd manage.

'All right. You win,' she said in a defeated voice. 'I'll do whatever you want.'

He raised a sardonic brow.

'Only as far as work goes,' she amended icily. 'I don't intend to give you complete rights over me.'

'No? I can't guarantee that I won't find your continued presence…enticing. There's something about you that excites me. I must go for the "madonna-harlot" type.'

His words had set up a low warmth in her body. He knew exactly what tone of voice to use when he wanted to be sultry, she thought resentfully.

'Touch me ever again and I'll make sure it's a long time before you're able to walk again!' she threatened.

He laughed, desire remaining in his eyes, and to Lucy he looked devilish. She could imagine him doing anything to get whatever he wanted. He wasn't a man she should underestimate, ever. She locked that thought away in her mind, to remember for the future. Something told her that they would have frequent clashes over the next couple of days.

'You will work from nine to six o'clock, seven days a week. Lunch will be a one-hour break. On Sunday you will be given time off to visit the small chapel in the *palazzo* if you wish to attend,' he said crisply.

Brute! No wonder Selina hated it here. But Lucy wasn't afraid of hard work, and she'd worked longer hours at the Home. She'd show him; his intended harsh regime wouldn't get her down. Though she didn't expect to be on the island for long. Selina would be in touch.

'You go to church in England?' he asked.

'What?' Maybe he was trying to find out if she was a decent kind of person, after all. 'Yes, every Sunday. I push old Mrs Baker in her wheelchair and...'

'I don't want to hear,' he said roughly, making her dislike him more than ever. Too many people found old, infirm men and women a nuisance. 'I wouldn't have thought you believed in God.'

'Well, I do,' she answered in a low, hurt tone.

'Then,' he said triumphantly, unchaining a book from a library shelf, 'you will swear on my family Bible that you won't go ashore without my permission and my knowledge.'

'Clever,' said Lucy sarcastically.

'I thought so.' He gave a wintry smile. 'If I'd asked you straight out to swear on the Bible, I'd never have known whether you meant it or not. By the way, there will be plenty of people keeping an eye out for you, in case you decide to break your promise. You can travel to the other islands freely, although you won't have much spare time, of course. But don't go to the mainland.'

'What is the salary?' she asked sullenly.

'You'll earn good money. Though I'll have to retain it all.'

'My earnings? Why?' she cried, her hopes of gathering some money together for her ticket completely dashed.

'I'm owed a great deal. You are my insurance,' he answered silkily.

'I can never repay the money that's missing!' She was horrified: did he intend to keep her here for ever? Supposing Renzo and Selina had decided never to return?

'No. That's why I'm sure you'll do everything you can to see that your sister appears with the money. I guarantee her freedom if she does, providing she leaves Renzo alone,' he added harshly.

'But I keep telling you, I don't know where she is!' wailed Lucy.

'Maybe. But do you think she'll leave you here without trying to make contact? Is she that heartless?'

She didn't know. She didn't know anything at that moment except a feeling of total despair. It was impossible for her to stay long—certainly not the length of time he seemed to be envisaging. Temporary replacements were all very well, but they didn't take the place of someone who loved and understood the foibles and needs of each resident. Lucy's teeth dug deeply into her lip. Tears began to trickle slowly from the corners of her eyes, and she raised them appealingly to Max, her thick lashes wet and glistening.

'Promise,' he said thickly, thrusting the Bible at her.

The choice seemed to be between being instrumental in sending her sister to jail—which would kill her doting father—or getting hold of some money somehow and flying back to care for everyone in the Home before the replacement left. She'd have to use her wits. Banking on the fact that somehow the social services would cope and that no one would leave ten people incapable of

looking after themselves to their own fate, she reached
out blindly and placed her hand on the huge book.

'I s-s-swear,' she sobbed.

She heard it thud shut and Max move away.

'Stop crying,' he growled.

'I c-c-can't!'

'I'll leave you here to pull yourself together. When
you have, step on to the terrace.' He cleared his husky
throat. 'I'll have a uniform for you to change into. You
might as well learn about the job straight away.'

A door slammed and silence descended on the big
empty room. Lucy felt blindly for the chair and curled
up, giving vent to her distress, not caring that she had
no handkerchief and that tears were coursing down her
face unchecked, dropping warmly on to her chest.
Somehow she had to get out of this awful mess; somehow
she had to convince Mazzardi that he could trust her
and she'd always been acting with the best of intentions.

Doubts about Selina began to assail her and she fought
to explain them away, concerned at her lack of loyalty.
It was obvious that Mazzardi was a devil when crossed,
and Lucy could see that a series of foolish actions had
put her half-sister in a situation far more serious than
she'd ever envisaged. When they knew their love would
never be accepted, she and Renzo almost had to take
the money, in order to bribe their way across country
and hide for a while. Lucy brightened. Perhaps Selina
had already reached home!

She'd persuade Mazzardi that she must ring to check
everything was going smoothly, and would make some
kind of oblique reference when she spoke to mother or
Lionel. She rubbed her knuckles over her eyes and stood
up, looking for the door to the terrace and walking out
into the warm sun.

Max's dark, smudged eyes flickered towards her, coldly following the trail of tears. Lucy hastily covered her chest, her thumb touching the damp valley between her breasts. He obviously found her ravaged appearance so ugly that he immediately turned away.

'Your uniform is on the chair. Take it and wash your face in your room before you change. I want you down here, smart and composed, in fifteen minutes.'

Muttering under her breath, she grabbed the outfit and made to go back the way she'd come.

'The servants' stairs,' he said coldly. 'That direction. Remember? You used them once before, I imagine.'

'I am sorry, sir,' she said, innocent-eyed and trying to remember the exact words he'd used to deceive her. 'I've never done this kind of thing before. My first time, you know.'

'Don't be clever!' he thundered, spinning around, his eyes flashing danger signals.

'Sorry, sir. I'll cultivate humbleness if that gives you a kick.' Her eyes levelled with his. 'You might be able to use blackmail to keep me here against my will, but you won't crush me, I can promise that!'

Lucy swept out, the tears dry now, proud and defiant, her bright cascade of hair swinging angrily, her hips jaunty in the tight-fitting dress. Max Mazzardi's eyes hungered after her till she had turned the corner of the building. Her confidence seemed born of honesty, yet that was impossible. She had deceived him with all the expertise of a practised courtesan. He set his teeth. How she would regret that!

CHAPTER SIX

THE uniform was flattering—in a smoky blue-grey, contrasting beautifully with the brilliance of Lucy's hair. The simple gored skirt had a linen look to it, and was very cool—already the attic bedroom felt hot and stuffy, despite the fact that the windows were still open as wide as they could go. Unable to see herself properly in the small mirror, she stood on tiptoe to judge the effect of the collarless top, with its short sleeves and wide belt, all matching the skirt.

Prim, neat and efficient. Selina would have hated it! Lucy smiled wryly, brushed her hair back severely from her face and tied it at the nape of her neck, improvising with a narrow silk scarf she found.

That would have to do. With the impatient Mazzardi waiting downstairs, she'd have to hurry if she was to meet his fifteen-minute deadline. Grumbling at all the stairs, she hurtled downwards, thinking how her sister must have disliked the poky little room and the long climb up to it every night after work.

When she rounded the corner of the building on her way to the secluded terrace, she saw that Max was lost in thought, striding up and down with his head lowered and his hands pushed into the pockets of his elegant trousers. It seemed to Lucy that his mood was blacker than his suit. Everything about him indicated a man in a temper; the clenched fists that stretched the material tightly across his thighs, the hard-heeled, thudding strides, the impatient rise and fall of his high, uncompromising shoulders and finally the sinister concentration on his face.

Lucy steeled herself and walked forwards, knowing that he'd had plenty of time to think of a thousand ways to make life difficult. It would take all her optimism and courage to survive the machinations of this man!

'It's a very attractive uniform, you chose well,' she said, deciding on her tactics. Men like him adored flattery.

'Not me. My father.' He looked at her sourly.

Lucy hesitated. 'Did you come here for his funeral?' she asked, remembering what Max had told her about his father's death, uncertain what parts of his story were true.

'I wasn't asked,' he said laconically. 'Not till later, when the inadvisability of relying on Renzo to take the reins became apparent. Let's get started. I have a lot to do.'

His tour was brisk and efficient, taking her around the vast rooms of the *palazzo* at a breakneck speed. She had panicked after a few minutes, thinking she'd never retain everything he was saying.

'Look, I don't know if you're doing this intentionally or not, but I can't remember everything. You're going too fast and saying too much. I haven't got that kind of memory,' she'd said firmly. 'If you want me to make a good job of this, I need a notebook or a tape recorder to take down what you tell me.'

'Don't worry. The last thing I want is another incompetent,' he said coldly. 'I propose to give you a brief feel of the place and then you'll follow me around as I guide the groups, picking up tips on how to handle questions, children with sticky fingers and so on. All the information has been printed out and you'll learn it in your spare time.'

'I'll have spare time?' she asked sarcastically.

He smiled. 'I could arrange that you don't,' he purred.

'No!' she said, shaking her head vigorously.

'You can spend your lunch hour collecting your things from the hotel,' he said, moving on to the next room.

'My things?' she asked stupidly, forgetting he didn't know she'd been cleaned out by Selina. 'Oh, yes, of course.'

'Pay your bill and bring your belongings straight back here, then be ready to start the afternoon session. There's one other English guide and he goes to lunch when you return, so don't keep him waiting as your thoughtless sister always did. You can flirt with the local men in your own time, not mine.'

Lucy had hardly heard any of his last remarks. Her mind was whirling with one word going around and around: *bill!* She had no money! Whereas before she'd worried about having enough to cover her personal needs and incidentals, and considered the idea of moon-lighting to save up for her ticket home, now she was in real trouble!

Max's yell from the next room brought her head up sharply. Impatient monster!

'Keep up with me,' he complained, returning to the connecting doorway. 'I'm in a hurry, you know that.'

'I—I——' She bit back her misery, determined not to cry, twisting her hands feverishly in the effort of control.

'What is it?' came his voice, more gentle and almost caring.

Dimly, through the blur of tears in her eyes, she could see his dark-clad figure a few inches away. 'I hate crying!' she sniffed. 'It's a useless thing to do!'

'Oh, I don't know,' he sighed, his hands warm and soothing on her shoulders. 'It seems to work on me.'

Startled, she looked up at him. He seemed to be as perplexed as she was. 'I don't know what to do or who to turn to,' she whispered. 'You refuse to accept that what I tell you is the truth, and obviously feel justified in putting me in an awful situation. I missed phoning home last night and I don't even know if they're managing. Don't you care that old Mrs Knight is disorientated without me? Don't you feel any responsibility for the fact that my elderly parents are worrying?'

To her relief, he looked stricken.

'I'm sorry,' he muttered. 'Ring them now.'

'Now?' she repeated, wide-eyed. 'But it's peak time——'

'Now, before I change my mind!' he rasped, turning her around and pushing her relentlessly towards a small office off the grand hall.

To her consternation, he stayed in the office, leaning negligently against the wall, his arms folded and a watchful expression on his face.

'If this is a trick, if you're lying,' he said softly, 'I'll make you wish you'd never been born.'

She searched hastily for the international dialling code, thankful that he didn't come over to help. He'd soon discover she was telling the truth. All the while she cross-examined Lionel about the residents, after greeting him with unabashed affection and warmth, she was conscious of Max's unfaltering gaze. That made it even more awkward for her to ask Lionel if she could stay a couple of extra days, but was reassured by her stepfather's generous reply. They could manage for a whole week without her chocolate cakes. Any more than that, and mutiny would break out. As Lionel described how the residents would be armed with domestic weapons, she found it hard to stop her lips from trembling.

'So you do run a Home,' said Max quietly, when she replaced the receiver.

'I told you,' she said in a choked voice. Everyone was missing her dreadfully, but all their needs were being well catered for. She'd managed to fudge over her answer about Selina's health, mumbling that she looked as lovely as always. Max had come to stand very close. He seemed to have no idea of personal space! She trembled a little at the breadth of chest in front of her eyes. His masculinity always caught her unawares.

'You sounded concerned,' he said.

'Of course,' she whispered. 'Surely you of all people with your business in someone else's hands, far away in England, must realise how I feel? And I have the added worry because I'm dealing with people I love and who are very dependent on me. Look, Max, I can understand how angry you must be and frustrated that Renzo isn't here so that you can get on with your own life, but it really isn't my fault. You must see that I can't stay here longer than the end of the week. That's when my stand-in goes to her next post.'

He gave a small wry laugh. 'Here we both are, on one of the most beautiful islands in the world, in warm sunshine, surrounded by exotic gardens, and we're both desperate to get back to rainy old England!'

She gave a weak smile. 'Ridiculous, isn't it? But—you do understand, don't you?'

'Yes,' he said quietly. 'I think I've misjudged you a little. Perhaps you acted in a misguided way. Time will tell. In the meantime, we must meet the first group.'

During the morning, Lucy discovered the charming side of Max as he expertly steered the visitors around his palace. In a remarkable mixture of good humour and authority, he fended off questions about the family, removed children from the high balconies above the lake, smilingly confiscated their chewing gum and answered hundreds of questions with unfailing patience. He was very different from the irritable, scowling and forbidding man she'd glimpsed earlier. But then, this was a job, and he was superb at business, less skilled, it seemed, in dealing with family.

She found it hard to concentrate, but did her best, knowing she'd be put to the test all too soon. So she tried to learn, hindered by Max's charismatic personality, which flowed out unchecked to everyone in the group, warm, interesting, making the whole palace come to life with his ancestors striding, mincing, fighting, and loving their way through the classically beautiful apartments.

'Isn't he a dish?' sighed a girl in the group of about Lucy's age. 'All that energy and passion—I bet he's a handful in bed!'

Lucy had smiled, and then blushed furiously because, in a brief silence, the girl's words were overheard by everyone in the group. She seemed quite unconcerned, grinning saucily at Max, whose laughing eyes were assessing Lucy's embarrassment.

After that, the group had teased him unmercifully, and even he was having difficulty controlling them. He breathed a sigh of relief as they departed to wander around the extensive gardens and flicked a raised eyebrow at her.

'Coffee?'

'Oh, yes, please,' she returned fervently.

He altered the clock to show the time of the next tour, and led her along a narrow path through tall, glossy-leaved magnolia trees. They had a blissful fifteen-minute break. She felt as if she'd been involved in a performance that had stirred up her adrenalin and left her pulses racing.

'I didn't realise there was audience participation,' she said, thankfully slumping in a deep basket chair.

'We're virtually producing a show here. Don't get too comfortable,' he warned, stretching a long arm out for a coffee percolator. 'We haven't long. Now, what do you remember? How long have the Mazzardis been here?'

'Since 1547,' she said, her mouth full of biscuit. This was supposed to be her coffee break!

'Tell me about the first public visitors,' he said relentlessly.

She sighed. 'Your grandparents first opened the house to tourists in... I forget the date. Your grandmother had taken a special interest in the gardens and insisted on placing fountains in such unsuitable sites that unsuspecting visitors were swamped when they were turned on and spent a couple of hours in the hothouse, drying off. It took a long time to persuade your grandmother to have the fountains re-sited.'

'Yes.' He smiled distantly. 'She's a very stubborn woman.'

'She's still alive?' asked Lucy curiously.

'She's single-minded enough to outlive us all,' he answered bitterly. His brows were knitted together in a solid black line.

A man in the distance began to throw out grain on to the lawn, which ran down to the water's edge, and brightly coloured parakeets appeared as if from no-where. She'd heard their chatter earlier, coming from the direction of one of the huge cedar trees. When she looked back at Max, he was more relaxed and smiling absently at the squabbling birds.

'It's so lovely here,' she said softly. 'I don't see how you could ever leave.'

'I didn't want to. I was driven out.'

'At the age of eighteen?'

He considered for a moment, before answering. 'Father and I had an argument about Renzo; one so bitter that I couldn't retract everything I'd said and nor could he. We'd gone too far. We were too alike, Father and I. Impatient, quick-tempered, needing to be boss, sure of our own supreme ability.'

'So what did you do?' she asked cautiously, fascinated by the insight—and impressed by his honest assessment of himself.

'It was obvious to me that I wasn't wanted. My brother was quite sufficient for everyone,' he said quietly. 'I took all my savings and flew to England. My English was pretty good and my knowledge of fine wines meant that I was able to find a job as a wine salesman. I learned, watched, planned, picking up as many skills as I could.' His face brooded at the memory. 'It was a hard life; lonely and alien. But I was determined to be successful. The only time I returned was when my mother was killed when her launch hit some floating logs. I soon returned to my own company. We export to the whole world now.'

No wonder he appeared ruthless, thought Lucy. He'd been without people to care for him for so many years.

'What's happening to your company while you're over here?' she asked.

'Heaven knows,' he said gloomily. 'I have a multi-million-pound business that revolves around me, and I'm trying to run it from the end of a telephone while I guide people around the estate with one hand because we're short of guides and try to go through Father's papers with the other.'

'Now I understand why you want Renzo back,' she said earnestly.

'Yes,' he growled. 'Until he turns up and I've sorted him out, I'm stuck here playing lord of the island and sorting out staffing problems, maintenance difficulties and trying to keep the auditors out of the books till the missing cash is replaced. And all the time, my firm, which I've sweated blood and tears over for the last ten years, waits quietly in the background. I built that firm! I'm proud of it!'

'Oh, Max,' she said, her face troubled and sympathetic, 'I'll do everything I can to get Selina back, I promise. The moment she contacts me, I'll tell you. We must work something out between us.'

'I think you mean that,' he said slowly.

'I do! Please believe me.'

'It's a tempting idea. In the meantime, drink up. You have your next group to accompany soon.' He stretched out his long legs. 'It's quite fun, in a masochistic way, isn't it?'

'I suppose so,' she said doubtfully.

He smiled at her expression. 'Wait till the coach parties turn up this afternoon. Then you'll really find out what repartee is like.'

'I'm dreading it,' she admitted, putting down her cup. 'I'm not used to selling myself, like you. Oh, I didn't mean...!'

'I know what you meant,' he grinned. Lucy fought to stop herself melting from his charm. 'You're not used to the public spotlight. Instead you hide yourself away, spending your whole life devoting yourself to others: serious, dedicated, ignorant...'

'Thank you very much,' she said crossly.

'Well, you are. I don't think you know the first thing about men below the age of retirement.'

'I'm not sure I want to, from what I've seen,' she said drily.

'What have you seen?' he asked gently. 'A man who never had the chance to beg his father's forgiveness before he died, who is trying to hold two wildly differing businesses together, placate a crotchety grandmother, find a runaway brother and his foreign mistress and the family jewels. You haven't exactly seen that man at his best, Lucinda.'

His eyes were confusing her. She felt a tremendous liking for him and tried hard to remember that he was blackmailing her. He was intending to use any trick he could to smash Selina's relationship with Renzo. She mustn't be fooled by his charm again.

'Time we went.' She pushed down the sensation of longing and stood up primly.

'Lucinda,' he said, catching her hand.

But she snatched it away and glared at him. 'I asked you not to touch me,' she said frostily.

'So you did,' he murmured.

He'd lost his sparkle, that was apparent on the next few tours. The women in the groups still found him devastatingly attractive, but it was a more remote and unobtainable Max Mazzardi who regaled them with the details of the *palazzo* and his ancestors.

Lucy had almost given up trying to unravel such a complex man. He'd said she didn't know much about men and he was right. Sometimes she thought he was a swine, and sometimes she felt unwillingly drawn to him, as if invisible links were being forged between them with every breath they took and every glance they exchanged.

She glowered at Max from under her lashes. He was pointing out the details on one of the sixteenth-century tapestries to his fascinated audience in his rich voice. He always became sensual when he discussed the Flemish tapestry, she mused absently. It was a subject dear to his heart.

'Perhaps the ladies here would like to examine this hanging,' he said, a curl of sexuality heightening the arch of his upper lip. 'This shows male vices. Gentlemen, over here is one depicting female vices. Incidentally, on the other side of the room are their counterparts, showing human virtues, but I'm sure you're not interested in them!'

A ripple of laughter ran around the visitors.

'What's going on there?' asked one woman, askance, peering at the tapestry. Max moved closer and was soon surrounded, murmuring quietly to the women.

It was the last room on the tour. Lucy suddenly had to get outside, to force her body into some action instead of letting it seethe with irrational anger at the attention he was giving the women. She couldn't conceive why her instincts were trying to acquire some kind of ownership over him. But the sight of him bending his handsome head to one female and then another had rent her inside.

She leaned back against the peach-coloured walls, warm from the sun, and closed her eyes. She mustn't find him attractive. He was so unsuitable. Every inch of him was heavy with sensuality while his brain stayed cold. She *was* too ignorant to handle men like that. She sighed. In a few days she'd be back to her normal duties. The only difference was that this experience of meeting Max had made her very, very restless. And she'd known the mental and physical ache that came when you wanted someone who was unobtainable and totally *wrong*.

'Tired?'

Her eyes shot open, to find Max's face unnervingly near. For a mad moment, she thought his lips had brushed her cheek, and then she dismissed the idea when he stood back and gave her a mocking smile.

'Is it lunchtime?' she asked breathlessly.

'It is. Dash over to Pescatori and sort everything out. You should have plenty of time to grab a snack when you come back. We provide slabs of pizza, pies, dishes of *lasagne al forno*, fruit, ice-cream, that sort of thing, in the same place we had coffee. You'll meet one or two of the other guides there, too.'

'And . . . what about you?' she blurted out.

'I have some paperwork to catch up on. Let's hope someone remembers to bring me something to eat today. I went without yesterday because I didn't notice it was lunchtime. Don't be late, remember. We'll meet at two, by the clock. If I'm not there, start without me.'

'Oh, I couldn't!'

'Don't worry, it's not a rendezvous I'm likely to forget,' he said gently. 'Go! Before I delay you any more!'

She stumbled hurriedly off, his chuckle following her, and then remembered.

'Max!' she cried anxiously.

In a flash, he had spun on his heels and was striding towards her, suddenly powerfully certain of himself. Lucy felt her knees buckle as his intention became clear, and she tried to clear her throat to speak but the words wouldn't come.

'Lucinda,' he muttered, slowly, painfully slowly, drawing her towards him. He tilted up her chin with gentle, warm fingers, the tenderness of his touch and the indefinable message in his eyes mesmerising her. Her startled eyes, as soft as a frightened deer, were widening as the distance between their lips was decreasing. She fought her way out of the mental torpor.

'I don't have any money down here!' she gasped through dry lips. His whole body tensed. 'It'll take too long to go upstairs... can you lend me enough to get to the island and back?' Her heart was rocketing around in her ribcage, knowing that she'd made him angry. He'd been about to kiss her, something she wanted more than anything in the world, and she'd turned the moment into a plea for sordid cash! He'd never forgive her, never, but it had saved her from foolishness.

His fingers slid to the small of her back and pressed hard so that she was forced against his chest. In vain she tried to avoid the intimacy of his thighs. Every one of his muscles was tensed, and she believed that she was in contact with almost all of them. A flood of heat surged into her body, settling indecently in a blazing fire that merged with the throbbing heat of his loins. She clenched her jaw at the raw sexuality of her own body, urging her to stupidity.

'What's it worth?' he growled.

From a determined study of his tie, she flicked her lashes up at him in astonishment.

'Worth a quick kiss, surely?' he drawled. 'And don't look so shocked. It's no more than your sister suggested.'

'W-w-what——'

'Time is running out,' he mocked. 'Do you prefer to run all the way up to the attic for your purse, or will you kiss me for the fare? Come on, Lucinda, I want to know how far you'll go to stay as pure as you say you are.'

'You're the devil himself!' she breathed, desiring his mouth, knowing she was lost.

'So I've been told,' he grated with satisfaction, lowering his dark head.

CHAPTER SEVEN

IF IT had been a bruising, callous kiss, one of punishment and scorn, she could have withstood it; hating him for not being the kind of man she dreamed of. But his mouth swept warm and tenderly across her lips, as soft and coaxing as a lover's eyes. Lucy made a little sound of despair in her throat, and the kiss deepened, yet still was gentle. And so incredibly sweet was the taste of his lips that she found her arms slipping up his powerful chest and linking around his neck.

He froze and her eyes snapped open as their lips reluctantly separated.

'Max,' she whispered, appalled at the anguish she saw.

'Take the money,' he rasped, pushing her away and thrusting notes into her pocket. 'For goodness' sake, get out of my sight!'

She turned away immediately with a choking sob and began to run. He thought she was without morals. She'd almost convinced him of her innocence, and then she had to go and ruin it all by asking for money and responding to his kiss! He was right. She was ignorant of men—but she longed to be taught everything by him, whatever it eventually cost her in a broken heart, however awful it was when he finally tired of playing around with someone he obviously saw as a willing sacrifice in his efforts to arouse his jaded appetite. It was all so unfair!

She would show him that she was to be respected by calmly rejecting him. She had to, otherwise he'd never think she was honourable and trustworthy. For Selina's sake, she had to stay aloof in order to convince him that they had both been brought up with high moral standards. What on earth would he think of her if she sank into his arms every time he raised his eyebrows enquiringly at her?

Max was unobtainable. Some women could leap straight out of their backgrounds into another. Selina could. She had the courage and style to enter the world of the Mazzardis because she had plenty of confidence and more than a touch of innocent arrogance. Lucy wondered what Max would think of spending an evening in the kitchen at Park View, sipping hot chocolate, or helping her to push Mrs Baker down to the bowling green and giggle at her outrageous criticisms.

Lucy grinned. That was better! She'd swept away any lingering, wistful dreams. One day she'd tell her sister how Max had flirted casually with her and they'd both laugh. Her eyes grew serious again as she acknowledged quietly to herself that she could never discuss him. What had happened was private and rather humiliating. If Selina and Renzo did stay together, there would be a few awkward moments in the future, when she and Max met again. Though she could imagine him being totally controlled and icily pleasant.

'Isola dei Pescatori!' bellowed a deck-hand, over the loudspeaker.

Lucy jumped. In a moment she was hurrying over the gangplank and weaving her way through the holidaymakers, bound for the Hotel Borromeo.

'Ah, good day, Miss Parish!' beamed the *patrone* when she hesitantly entered the hall. 'We think you gone. No dress, no wash face things!'

'Oh!' She'd forgotten the cleaners would find out. 'I— I'm working for Signor Mazzardi,' she said hastily. 'I moved in last night.' Thank goodness she could tell the truth! 'If any messages come, telephone calls, letters, can you send them to Isola Mazzardi for me?'

'Yes, yes. I do this. Good, is good. I see this.' He pointed to her uniform as if he recognised it. 'You like the bill now?'

'No, that is...' Lucy was not used to delaying payments, and this was deeply embarrassing. 'I can't pay you,' she blurted out in shame. 'Not until I have made some money.'

He frowned, all smiles gone. 'You pay.'

Mentally cursing Selina, Lucy nodded emphatically. 'Yes, I will. I promise. My...' Oh, this was awful. 'My money is delayed,' she continued shakily, trying not to lie. A distortion of the truth wasn't too wicked, was it? 'My money is coming.'

He pursed his lips, studying her unhappy face intently. Then he nodded. 'You have good face. I am mad, but I see you feel bad inside. You shake the hand, yes?'

She nodded dumbly, intensely humiliated at being in debt, and blessing the consummate generosity of the easy-going Italian. How could Selina do this to her? She vowed never to fully trust her again.

'Perhaps I could pay more quickly if I worked for you. An evening job. Can you help?'

To her dismay, he shook his head slowly. 'I have nothing. You go down road,' he suggested, waving his arms at the little path that ran along the shore. 'Cafés. You go.'

The telephone interrupted him, and with more gestures and nods to her he started a voluble conversation, leaving Lucy with no alternative but to try elsewhere.

Clustered around the small jetty where the ferries called, were small and colourful *trattoria*, jutting into the lake like piers, giving the customers wonderful views of the shimmering mountains and busy water-traffic as little boats plied to and fro. By the time she had tried all but the last two cafés on the island, she was hot and sticky—and running out of time.

Mercifully one needed a waitress and washer-up. No one seemed to worry at her lack of Italian, and she supposed it was because the clients were multinational and the menu was in three languages anyway. If she worked overtime and tips were reasonable, she could pay off the hotel. That meant she was relying on some kind of contact from Selina if she was to get home.

On the ferry back, she tried not to think of the awful times ahead. On top of acting as guide for Max, she'd be working till the early hours of the morning. It was just as well she was tough and had plenty of energy. Lucy sighed. Being on her feet constantly was a little different from having the opportunity to do a few jobs sitting down. And although she was virtually on call all through the night if necessary, she did go to bed early and usually managed to sleep heavily in between the odd night-time demands. Maybe it wouldn't be for long. Once Selina stopped thinking about her own plight and re-alised the situation she'd left behind, she'd send the money back.

It was late; too late to eat anything. The search for work had taken longer than she'd expected. She sat under the shaded awning on the boat returning to Isola Mazzardi, trying to cool down and calm down, telling herself that worrying wouldn't help. Her uniform was sticking to her and she'd caught the sun on her face and arms, which made her feel uncomfortable. She undid her top button and let the breeze from the ferry's motion cool her down a little.

Grimly she raced up the steep steps towards the gathering point where the tours started, only to find the first one of the afternoon had begun.

Max saw her immediately she joined the group. For a brief second his eyes blazed at her, and then he turned his disdainful shoulders and led everyone on to the next room. For the next hour, she fought to learn facts, miserably aware that he was deliberately avoiding eye-contact with her. Finally the group dispersed to the gardens and she was standing behind Max, his broad back telling her everything she needed to know. They were alone on a patio. In the silence, she felt apprehensive.

'Explain.'

She stared at the uncompromising width of his angry shoulders. 'It took longer than I thought. I'm sorry,' she said quietly.

He whirled around, his face dauntingly bleak. 'Look, I know this isn't going to be your career, and I know that you have as much interest in the work as your sister, but I warn you: if you're late again, I'll prevent you from leaving even this island.'

'Oh, no! You can't!' she cried, aghast.

'How else am I to ensure you meet your obligations? Hell, I was a fool to think you had a sense of responsibility.'

'I do,' she insisted. 'I didn't want to be late. I couldn't help it.'

Max's eyes glittered black and hard. 'How often do you think I heard that excuse from your sister?' he asked. 'Spoken with the same degree of innocent despair?'

Lucy hung her head. So much for impressing Max with her good character. 'Sack me if you must,' she said listlessly. 'At least that will get me away from you.'

He flinched and she was glad, glad that it hurt him to discover there was a woman in this world who wasn't prepared to overlook his overbearing manner and cold heart because of his compelling masculinity.

'I won't sack you. I didn't even sack Selina,' he said in a low tone.

'If she was so awful as you keep making out, why didn't you? I can't see you tolerating anything but perfection,' she remarked.

'And give Renzo even greater cause to comfort her?' he scorned. 'I'm far more subtle than that. I tried to give her every opportunity to give in her notice. It was my intention to drive her away.'

'You succeeded,' said Lucy angrily.

'Yes. I hadn't expected her to persuade Renzo to go with her,' he growled. 'But now I have you. Don't slack, or I'll make sure you fall into bed too exhausted to feel like practising your wiles on anyone.'

'That's not fair!' she said hotly.

'In addition,' he continued, ignoring her outburst, 'if you dare to turn up and trail around again with a group in Mazzardi uniform, looking anything but neat and composed, I'll personally smarten you up. And that, if you're wondering, will entail hauling you into my bathroom, stripping and showering you and chopping off that wild-looking hair!'

'You wouldn't!' cried Lucy, trying to re-tie her ribbon, flustered that thick waves had escaped and were dipping on to her face.

'Try me,' he said grimly. His gaze challenged hers and then his hand snaked out and caught the fabric of her uniform at the neck, his fingers cool on her hot skin. Holding her eyes mockingly, he carefully slid the button into its buttonhole, allowing his hand to trail slowly and insultingly down the front of her jacket till she took a startled step backwards. 'Just try.' His voice had become soft and menacing, and there was a disturbing carnal look in his dark eyes. 'Back to work—and pay attention. You'll be on your own tomorrow and I'll be following your groups, listening to every word you utter.'

'Brute!' she muttered, quelling the shocking dart of excitement that flared in her chest. He was a mean, venomous man and no mistake!

'On the contrary,' he drawled. 'I'm restraining myself. I advise you not to cross me. I could make life very unpleasant for you if I wished.'

'I always maintain,' she retorted, glaring at him, 'that the strong should support the weak. Through no fault of my own I'm in your power. Only a swine would take advantage of that situation. What an unpleasant man you are!'

To her astonishment, he flinched. 'You don't understand,' he muttered.

'Explain!' she demanded, mocking him with his own word.

'There isn't time,' he said with irritation.

'No time? Always you complain about punctuality. Were you a clockwatcher before you left home?' she scorned.

'Damn you!' he rasped. 'First, the public have a right to expect that a tour at three o'clock actually begins then. Second, if each group is a few minutes late then it clashes with every other tour going on: another English one, two German and two Italian. We'd all be bumping into each other. Third, we'd all finish work late—and you might have nothing to do in the evenings, but I have. This place has to run like clockwork. *Capisci?*'

She understood that kind of efficiency: there were periods during the day when she had to work like a machine in the Home if everyone was to be bathed and fed. Her daily helper had complained once, until Lucy had explained.

'I'm sorry. You're right, and I shouldn't have tried to score points off you. It's just...well, you make me so...'

'Me too,' he agreed. 'You make me so...'

She gave a sad half-smile and he glowered at her. 'You're trying to get round me again,' he muttered.

'No,' she said quietly, her hazel eyes trying to tell him that she was guileless.

His expression had softened and then, disappointingly, he withdrew behind his cynical barricade. 'I think,' he said slowly, his eyes hooded, 'that it would be better if you studied the notes for the rest of this afternoon. Find a quiet place in the gardens. In fact ... go into the private section. You know where it is. I can't go on doing this job, I have far too much desk-work untouched. You really will have to take over tomorrow, and you need to have all the facts at your fingertips.'

With a dismissive gesture, he strode away towards the meeting point. She looked at the sheaf of notes in her hand and turned with a sigh towards the private garden which she had never entered before.

Max must be at his wits' end, she thought. Everyone was relying on him: the people he employed in his own business, the people here, and his family. The responsibility was horrendous, and wasn't made any easier with the possibility of a family scandal.

Gradually, in the midst of her concern, she became aware of the beauty and silence of the garden. Huge rhododendron bushes and a screen of trees made it completely private. She began to take an interest in the plants, trying to identify them: the fragrant citrus, a delicate mimosa, the incense plant—what was its name?

A smile flitted across her lips when she emerged from an avenue of camphor trees and saw a small lake enclosed by an oleander hedge and resplendent with tall water-lilies with huge, exotic flowers the colour of pearls. And there, by a bench, were two pure white peacocks, being fed by an elderly lady in a shabby black outfit and wispy hair who had obviously strayed in here by mistake, judging by the carrier bag and the sandwiches in her hand.

Lucy thought she'd better put the lady on the right track. 'Hello.' She smiled. 'This is private. *Privato.*'

'What?'

Lucy gently took her elbow, glad that she was English. 'It's private here.'

'I know. Nice, isn't it?'

Just like Mrs Baker! Lucy laughed. 'Shall I show you out?' she offered.

'Why? Is it going to rain? Who are you?'

'Lucinda. I'm a guide for the *palazzo.*'

'Help me to that seat. My legs aren't doing what I want them to,' she complained.

It wouldn't matter if the old lady stayed for a short while. She certainly seemed unsteady. They both sat down and smiled at the view. It had that effect on both of them.

'Lovely, isn't it?' sighed Lucy.

'Leaves can be a nuisance,' came the startling reply. 'Gardeners' nightmare. See this?' She reached out and tapped the mimosa leaves on the bush beside them. To Lucy's delight, they curled up like the hand of a smacked child.

'The sensitive mimosa!' exclaimed Lucy, trying for herself and laughing with the old lady at the shy plant's response. 'I ought to be reading through my notes,' said Lucy awkwardly. 'I have to learn all about the Mazzardi family.'

'Families! A curse and a joy. I have lost both my grandchildren,' she said sadly.

'Oh, I'm so sorry.' Lucy's heart went out to the old lady and, to take her mind off her sorrow, decided to chat about the garden at home. Soon, before she knew it, she was answering questions about Lionel and her mother and describing something of her routine.

Then one of Max's manservants came hurrying down the path to spoil it all. For a short while, Lucy had enjoyed being with the old lady. It was almost like being home and talking to everyone there. The summons from Max brought her back to reality.

He gave a brief, courteous bow of his head and, in deference to the elder woman, addressed her.

'Mr Mazzardi requests you join him in the salon.'

'Oh, dear,' sighed Lucy, 'that's the owner. You've been trespassing, I'm afraid, and I've been encouraging you. Don't worry, I won't let him yell at you.'

'I'm so glad,' said the old lady, allowing the manservant to carry her bag of sandwiches.

They were taken through high french doors into a small, intimate room which Lucy hadn't seen before. Max began to rise from a richly brocaded chair, but Lucy was already beginning to defend her actions before he even opened his mouth.

'Look, Max, I know I should have been studying and this lady isn't supposed to be in the gardens, but she did no harm. If you want to complain, then do so to me. Let her leave with dignity.'

'Such a kind girl,' beamed the old lady, patting Lucy's arm. 'Those peacocks are getting fat,' she said sternly to Max.

Lucy drew in her breath. Tact wasn't the dear lady's greatest virtue! Max folded his arms.

'I'm not surprised, if you wilfully feed them bread,' he observed.

'I'll do as I please.' Much to Lucy's embarrassment, the old lady shuffled over to an elegant chaise-longue and gingerly sat down.

Lucy walked closer to Max. 'You're to be nice to her,' she whispered out of the corner of her mouth.

'Why the hell should I? She's sabotaging the peacocks. Perhaps I'd better divert her and offer her some tea.'

He was being scornful, of course, pretending that he would entertain the shambling old dear. 'Please don't make fun of her!' Lucy muttered.

'I wouldn't dare,' he whispered back.

'What's going on?' demanded the old lady impatiently. 'I don't like it when people whisper.' She looked up to see a maid wheeling in a trolley of tea. 'Splendid! I like a little something at this time,' she confided to Lucy, ignoring Max. Lucy shot a helpless glance at him, but his expression was a blank. 'There's no gin. I like a little tot. Bring me some.'

Max stopped Lucy from saying anything by grasping her arm. He shook his head at the maid who left.

'Tea is much better for you. Don't you remember that the doctor forbade alcohol, Grandmamma?'

Lucy froze. Was he using that word in its proper sense, or to poke fun? Her wary eyes flicked between the two of them. The old lady did look at home in her surroundings, but that didn't mean anything.

Max gave a small smile at her confused face. 'Haven't you two met properly?' he asked smoothly. 'Grandmamma, this is Lucinda Parish. Lucinda, Contessa Daphne Mazzardi.'

Lucy went a bright pink as she shook hands with the Contessa. She'd made a fool of herself in Max's eyes again. He was a beast, not making the situation clear straight away.

'Parish,' said the Contessa. 'Not related to that nice Selina Parish?'

'My sister,' beamed Lucy. Someone was on their side, then!

'Different, aren't you?'

'Yes, I'm the plain one.'

'You? No, my dear. You're the one with the beauty. Lovely smile. You remind me of Renzo. Dearest Renzo,' her voice became wistful. 'Such a handsome boy. The image of my husband. Same name, too. My favourite grandson.'

Lucy was shocked at the blatant denial of Max. Aware of his tensed body, she knew he was hurt but didn't know what to say.

'Drink your tea, Grandmamma,' he said coldly.

'Don't try to boss me around. Shouldn't you be escorting the visitors now? I hope you're not going to prove unreliable. Since you made my Renzo leave with Selina, it's up to you to replace her until you find someone else.'

Max's jaw tightened. He seemed to be trying to control his temper. Lucy wished she didn't have to witness this scene.

'You complained that I never spent any time with you,' observed Max. 'Here I am. Jed has offered to do this shift for me. He heard you nagging me at breakfast. It seems, Grandmamma, that you are determined to pick fault with everything I do. I have done nothing right since I arrived.'

'You always were a difficult boy. Not like Renzo. He was——'

'I don't think this is something to discuss right now,' said Max tightly.

The Contessa rose, with sudden surprising dignity that transcended the shabby clothes and untidy hair. 'I don't want any more tea,' she said bitterly. 'Not with you. Not until you've found my grandson and begged his forgiveness. Then you can beg mine, for telling me that he took my jewels. As if he would! When he returns, you must leave, you and your vindictive nature!' She turned to the distressed Lucy. 'Don't get mixed up with this man. He's heartless. Take it from one who knows.'

She left and Lucy bit her lip. Max looked terribly upset. His hands were shaking as he poured himself more tea, and she felt compassion at the way he tried to pretend everything was all right and his grandmother's words hadn't hurt him.

'I apologise for my grandmother's forthright behaviour,' he said stiffly.

'Old people can be like that,' said Lucy. 'Sometimes they're careless about things they say, overemphasising, imagining people understand what they mean...'

'What are you trying to say?' he asked quietly.

'I'm sure she thinks highly of you and all you've done. She must!'

'No, she doesn't,' he said shortly. 'She's never forgiven me for announcing that I wasn't going to run the business here. It was her beloved husband's dream to create the gardens for the public to view, and she couldn't understand why I was apparently not interested. She's

English, as you will have gathered. Gardens are a passion with her. She was shocked that I could leave.'

'That's not the only reason for the bad blood between you,' commented Lucy.

'No,' he admitted. 'Some of it was my fault. They all doted on Renzo, you see. He'd been a delicate child and, while I was sent away to school at an early age, he had a governess at home. I'd return, tell them about things I'd done, and they'd be distracted about Renzo's cold hands, or his pallor...oh, a thousand things. It didn't matter what I did, how hard I tried, I became more and more alienated. Finally I had that blazing row with Father about the way Renzo was mollycoddled, and decided to cut all ties and start a new life.'

'And Renzo was groomed to take over instead?'

'Not really. Father wouldn't delegate. Renzo knew very little of what was going on, even though he was supposed to. I understand that he preferred to spend his time with his friends rather than work.'

'How sad. So he couldn't cope,' said Lucy sympathetically.

'He panicked at the responsibility. No one had ever given him a chance, I suppose,' said Max thoughtfully. 'He's been spoilt. It's not his fault—just makes it difficult for others to pick up the pieces.'

'I know,' said Lucy fervently. 'Same with Selina. People see her as a dizzy blonde, too precious to soil her hands. She's not really like that, either; she hasn't had a chance to be herself rather than what everyone else expects her to be.'

'That's generous of you. She zips around the world spending money and getting into trouble, and you stay at home, slaving away.'

'I told you,' she said. 'That's what I'm cut out for.'

'Maybe no one's given *you* a chance to be yourself,' murmured Max.

Lucy felt the treacherous warmth creeping into her bones. 'Excuse me,' she said. 'I must learn these notes. Thank you for tea.'

'Pleasure. Lucinda—I think it might be an idea if we continue this discussion. I've learnt quite a lot about you this afternoon. Why don't we have dinner? Perhaps in Stresa?'

There was nothing she'd like better. But already she desired him. Liking him would be fatal. Somehow she knew that she was perilously close to that.

'No, thank you,' she said casually, not meeting his eyes. 'I already have an engagement.' Serving a few hundred tourists, she thought.

'And...tomorrow?'

If only his voice weren't so darned husky! Lucy bit her lip in an effort to turn her attention from the little darts of pleasure at his invitation.

'I'm fully booked up.'

'Don't let it interfere with your work,' he snapped.

Lucy didn't turn to look at him, knowing his face would be hard and hiding the fact that he was offended that any woman could turn him down. She strolled out of the room and then ran upstairs to memorise the notes.

Lucy felt very tired at the end of the day, and her head reeled from the information she was trying to remember. Max had told her that dinner was very early, which was a relief to hear. At first she'd imagined that when she finished at six o'clock she would have to miss the evening meal if she was to be at the *trattoria* by seven-thirty. Apparently most of the staff lived out and only a handful stayed, taking the meal after a brief shower and a change of clothes.

Once again, she was faced with an impossible choice when it came to dressing, and was almost tempted to wear her grubby blouse and skirt. But they looked too awful. Conscious that dinner started at six-thirty, she rummaged through Selina's clothes and found a navy day dress that wasn't too low-cut. It was impossible to see its effect very clearly, though it did seem to cling rather lovingly to her body, and Lucy wished for the hundredth time that Selina had left at least two decent dresses.

As she tried on a pair of high heels, anxious to give her feet a change and not wear the old shoes she'd tramped around in all day, there was a knock on the door.

'Lucinda, are you ready? I've been sent to collect you.'

She laughed at herself and her reaction. She'd thought it was Max, up to his tricks again, and her heart had pounded violently. This was a younger, lighter voice, with none of Max's rich throaty sensuality.

'Hello,' she said on opening the door.

'Jed White,' said the grinning freckled man at the door. 'Max made me the head prefect for the day; showing the new girl where to go. I must say,' he said admiringly, his eyes popping as they toured her figure, 'he didn't say you were a mature student.'

Lucy laughed at him, enjoying his teasing. Somehow his glance didn't have the same... She lowered her lashes at her own wayward mind. She'd almost said 'delicious' sexual threat!

'We all eat together,' he chattered. 'Max doesn't stand on ceremony. Says we're all a team, working for the same end. Shocked one or two people after the formality of his father's days, I can tell you.'

It wasn't until they swept down the grand staircase and into the state dining-room that she understood what he meant. The huge table was still as it had been during the day, glittering with faceted glass and silver. But now it also groaned with steaming dishes and was surrounded by noisy people, all of whom were dressed like Jed in casual jeans and T-shirts.

She was welcomed pleasantly, and Jed found her a place next to him. Max, in a black shirt open at the neck and black trousers, had looked up briefly and then continued a discussion with Paolo, his manservant. Shooting a quick glance at them from under her lashes, it seemed to Lucy that they were arguing good-naturedly about something.

'Likeable man, isn't he?' commented Jed, passing her a huge dish of lasagne. 'No wonder he's a wine baron. I should think he'd make a success of anything he tackles. Mind you, he has his work cut out here. Quite a task he's taken on. It can't be easy, throwing up everything you've worked for all your life, to preserve the family inheritance.'

'I suppose not,' she said slowly.

'We don't reckon he'll stay. The old Contessa continually criticises him. Makes me mad. Once his brother comes back from holiday he'll hand over. Can't say I relish that—I'd rather Max ran the place. He gave us a brilliant pep-talk when he arrived. Very good at man-management.'

'I'm sure he is,' smiled Lucy ruefully, thinking his management also extended to women. 'But you can't like working for him, surely? Isn't he rather callous and bad-tempered?' she probed.

'No. Mind you, he shoots straight from the hip if he senses any abuse of privileges,' said Jed cheerfully. 'He doesn't tolerate slacking. That's why I can't understand him wanting his brother to take over.'

'What do you mean?' she asked, intrigued.

'Everyone knows Renzo was milking the place while the old man was still alive.' He looked around and lowered his voice, putting his head close to Lucy's. 'Renzo's a bit of a baddie.'

'Haven't you got the brothers mixed up?' she whispered.

'Good lord, no! Max is the one who sticks to his honour. He's tough, but you can rely on him to be just and fair. Renzo created chaos in the last few months while his father was dying. No one was paid properly, incorrect deductions were made and it was obvious that he preferred to spend his time gadding around instead of managing the island. Max is still frantically trying to unravel the mess. One or two of us have hinted that Renzo had his fingers in the till, but got the thick edge of his tongue.' Jed flashed a grin at Lucy and leaned even closer. 'I was on the receiving end of the tongue-lashing,' he whispered. 'Terrified me. I decided to let him find out for himself that his brother was a thief when he finally got to the accounts. Won't be long now, the way he's burning the midnight oil. Judging from his vehement defence of Renzo, he has no idea. It'll hit him like a thunderbolt.'

It all made sense now. It *was* Renzo who'd stolen the money and the jewels, not Selina. Renzo had led her sister astray with lies and glittering promises. The silly, impressionable girl! Her dismayed face turned almost instinctively to Max, a feeling of sympathy welling inside her.

His expression killed it instantly. He was looking at her as if she was dirt. Distressed, she tore her eyes away and pushed at her food, unable to taste it any more because of the lump in her throat. What had she done now?

All through the fish course, she ate like an automaton, listening to the happy chatter around, wondering why she alone merited the disapproval of the man at the head of the table. She checked her watch and realised she couldn't stay for the pudding, even if she'd been able to eat it without choking. She had to leave for work. Maybe while she was serving it would be possible to think of a plan to prevent Selina from being mixed up irretrievably with Renzo. Or...maybe she ought to tell Max the whole story and throw herself on his mercy.

The next thing she had to do was borrow some more money so she could get to Pescatori. How she hated doing this! It was a mystery to her how Selina could ask so casually for cash. For Lucy, the effort was a horrific ordeal.

'Jed,' she whispered, leaning near.

'Yup?' he whispered in conspiratorial fashion, making her giggle nervously.

'I—I need the ferry money to get to Pescatori. I was staying there at the hotel, and...' Deliberately she let her voice trail away, hoping he'd think her purse was there. 'I can pay you when I see you in the morning. I hate to ask...'

'No problem,' he said airily, digging into his pocket. 'Sure that's all you need?'

'Oh, yes,' she said thankfully. 'I'm terribly grateful.' She flung him one of her beautiful smiles.

Jed patted her hands which clutched the money in her lap. 'It's not exactly a fortune,' he murmured, his eyes smiling at hers. His hands remained on hers.

'You're very kind. Thank you. Excuse me, I'll be late! See you tomorrow,' she whispered.

As she crossed the hallway, footsteps sounded behind her. A glance over her shoulder confirmed her suspicions that Max was following her and she began to run, her feet clattering noisily on the marble floor. But he easily overtook her at the main door.

'Just a minute!' He placed his hands on either side of her against the door, effectively trapping her. 'What's going on between you and Jed?' he demanded.

'What?' She turned an astonished face up to his cold eyes.

'I saw how quickly you had him dancing attendance on you,' he breathed. 'I haven't seen such an exhibition of intimacy at my dinner-table since your sister's time! And what the hell was he doing with his hands under the table?'

Lucy couldn't think of an answer: anything she said would incriminate her. And she couldn't go into long explanations. She had to get away or she'd be late!

'I don't know what you mean,' she said coldly. 'We were just talking——'

'It looked more like kissing, his face was so close to yours,' he hissed.

She shook her head impatiently. 'Max, he was telling me something confidential——'

'Like where his room is?' he demanded, hard and bitter.

'Of course not!'

'What, then?'

'I told you, it was confidential.'

'Demanding money again? This time you managed to get payment in advance, I see,' he bit out. 'Does the kiss come later, or was the loan worth more than that?'

Her hand reached up to slap his face as blind fury erupted within her, but he was too quick and knocked her hand away.

'I need to know what's going on under my roof. Are you going to his room?' he growled.

'No, I'm not! I'm going to Pescatori.'

'What for? Who did you meet at lunchtime? Is that why you were so late—and so dishevelled?'

'This is extraordinary! No, I didn't meet anyone. I'd just been hurrying so some bad-tempered despot didn't yell at me because I was late! You have to believe that I don't behave like that.'

'Why should I? Your actions belie your words again. After all, you met a boatman one lunchtime and agreed to have a drink with him that same night.'

'That . . .' She frowned in exasperation. 'That was different,' she finished lamely.

He gave a disbelieving laugh. 'I don't know why I bother. Have an enjoyable evening,' he said, his nose and mouth curving in disgust. 'Try not to oversleep. Breakfast is at seven-thirty. Sharp!' he barked, making her jump.

'I'll be there,' she said, tipping up her chin and reaching for the huge gilt door-handles.

'I admire your stamina,' he said in a monotone.

Lucy stared at him with stricken eyes, inexplicably upset that he should think so badly of her. She desperately wanted his approval, but hadn't time to explain.

'Don't turn that look on me!' he growled.

With a gasp of frustration, she spun on her heel and raced out.

Max thudded the doors shut behind her.

CHAPTER EIGHT

IT WAS three o'clock in the morning before she returned to Isola Mazzardi. All evening she had made an effort to do her job well and to be charming and helpful, knowing that she was relying on tips to bump up her wages. Her feet hurt because she'd forgotten to change out of the high heels, and she found that instead of having freedom to think while she was washing up, her brain was too tired to function.

Damn Selina! she thought furiously, surprising herself by the force of her irritation as she waited an hour for the ferry. She stumbled over the pontoon at Isola Mazzardi and up the steps, half asleep, teetering in the heels, pausing occasionally from sheer exhaustion. Selina's clinging dress had gone down well with the customers, but she'd hated the way her walk had of necessity become hip-swinging, and now as she climbed the steps she hitched up the material above her knees to give herself freedom of movement.

The back of her neck pounded. Lucy pulled off her ribbon and ran her hands through her hair, massaging the nape of her neck in relief.

Then she turned around the bend and Mazzardi was standing at the top of the steps, big, solid and forbidding. Her knees buckled and she sat down weakly, unable to cope any longer, her hair tumbling about her face. She heard his measured tread coming inexorably nearer and swayed.

For a long, interminably nerve-racking time he simply stood beside her on the steps and gazed down. From the set of his body and his harsh breathing, she knew he was in an awful rage and she quailed, waiting for it to burst on her head. It wasn't any of his business what she did after working hours, but she just didn't have the energy to stand him ranting and raving at her. All she wanted was to crawl into bed and sleep.

'A bit too vigorous for you, was he?' he queried softly.

His words cut through her like knives. She made no answer, but sat shivering from exhaustion.

'Here.'

At the shaking voice, Lucy looked up slowly to the proffered hand and took it, allowing him to pull her on to her feet. The movement made her half fall towards him and he quickly grasped her shoulders, holding her away, as if he would be contaminated by touching her. The material of the dress was pushed off her shoulders by his movement and he gave a sharp, angry intake of breath as her pearly skin glowed in the moonlight.

Miserably she felt his hand around her waist, impersonally guiding her up the steps. A quick flicker of her lashes told her that he was seething.

'Just a minute,' she whispered, surprised at the huskiness of her voice. Carefully, as if her fingers were leaden, she reached into her pocket and counted out some coins. 'That's what I owe you,' she said, waiting for him to accept them.

'You…!' He reached out and swept them off her palm to the ground. The hand that warmed the small of her back slid around to grip her waist cruelly and she was hustled on, bewildered at his response. Then it dawned on her that he thought she'd been given the money by someone she'd met, that he'd imagined she'd earned it in a totally different way!

He actually thought she'd been...

Blackness swept over her, releasing her from the horror of the last few days. At last she felt suspended in peace and warmth, rested and free from her troubles. Yet it only seemed a short time before she was struggling against a long, slow climb back to wakefulness.

She was in her room and it was dark still, only the faint crescent moon filtering a little light on to the bed. She gave a groan and turned over, then screamed at the shadowy figure looming above her.

'Be quiet! It's me.' Max sank back to the chair which he'd drawn up beside the bed.

'You think that comforts me?' she croaked.

'Well, I'm one of the few people who won't attack you,' he muttered.

She passed a confused hand over her face and then was rigid with mortification. She'd remembered passing out in Max's arms—and now she was in bed...and in her underclothes!

'Who——' She licked dry lips. 'Who got me here?' she husked.

'I did.'

She swallowed and slid down in the bed, bringing the sheet up to her chin as if that would wipe out any knowledge he had of her body. All the time, she was wondering what he'd thought as he undressed her, if he'd paused and... Her eyes shut tightly. It was too awful to think about.

'How dare you undress me?' she said in a hoarse whisper.

'It was no pleasure, I assure you,' he grated. 'Now listen to me. I'm going to give you some advice—the same advice I gave Selina.'

'Keep your advice. I want to sleep,' she moaned, rolling over.

She gasped as rough hands hauled her round to face him again.

'Not yet,' he rasped. 'You'll listen. And you'll stop behaving like a slut. I don't think you realise how much you degrade yourself, Lucinda. Somewhere inside you is a decent woman, but every one-night stand you have is destroying that. For goodness' sake, stop burning the candle at both ends! I hate to see a woman cheapening herself like this.'

'Go away,' she muttered, her head woolly with lethargy.

Impatiently he hauled her into a sitting position, the sheet falling away and dragging down the lacy top of her bra to reveal her high, round breasts, soft-tipped with sleepiness. As his hungry eyes feasted on them, they stirred and tautened. Lucy gave a gasp of horror and covered herself quickly.

'Heaven save me—I want you!' he groaned, pushing her aside and straightening up.

Instantly a flame shot through her, lighting every nerve and firing each vein. Her body trembled under the raw desire in his pagan eyes, and then he had stormed out of the room, slamming the door behind him.

Defensively, she curled up in the bed, staring into the darkness. She wanted him too. The ache filled her loins with an insistent throb, but it was the ache in her heart that concerned her more. Max was the first man to arouse such deep and complex feelings within her, both sexually and emotionally. The desire between them was to be resisted with all her might. She couldn't proclaim her sister's morality from Max's bed! Not by a word or a gesture must she provoke him. A wicked thought flashed through her head: she *wanted* to provoke him beyond control. She wanted him to hold her, to kiss her till she was sated with his mouth.

A small moan escaped her lips. Max Mazzardi had turned her into a woman without shame. It was no use: whatever she told herself, she knew that she had fallen irrevocably for Max in the same way that Selina had fallen for his brother. Now she understood the desperation, the longing, the irrational behaviour that her sister had indulged in. You couldn't think straight when you were in love.

It was nearly five o'clock. She had two hours of sleep left. Shaking from utter exhaustion, she came to a decision. In the morning she would tell Max everything. Everything, that was, except the fact that she loved him. Once she did that, she would be totally in his power and his restraint would be swept away.

'Where's Max?' she hissed agitatedly at Jed, as they carried their plates of scrambled eggs and bacon on to the terrace where they'd lunched. Her bleary eyes took in the gossiping staff and the fact that Max was missing.

'Now, don't worry, you'll be fine,' soothed Jed.

'What do you mean?'

'Oh, I thought you were panicking about your duties! Didn't you see the schedules on the wall inside the door? You're doing the first tour at nine—that means you'll be finished at five. It gets easier the more you do it, and if you forget anything you always have the notes.'

'Isn't he here?' she persisted.

'No, left for Milan. He said he had some business there.'

Lucy gulped down the strong coffee, relieved that he wouldn't be present to see her first venture into guiding, and with a sensation of anticlimax that she couldn't clear up all the misunderstandings immediately. All through the day she worked hard, stumbling, striving, finding her own way of dealing with people and their queries, and trying to overcome the creeping tiredness that seeped into her bones.

At lunchtime she hurried over to the hotel and paid off some of her bill, and all through dinner she answered Jed's chatter absently, wishing Max would turn up. Somehow the place seemed less vibrant and exciting without him.

She managed quite well that evening, but was very shaky again when she finished in the early hours and slowly climbed the steps up to the *palazzo*. Suddenly they were lit by the searing white glare of a beam from a launch on the water. Her weary head turned to see that it was making its way to the small jetty, its powerful light sweeping the lake as the launch swerved to avoid a huge uprooted tree, half submerged in the inky water.

Lucy continued up, and when she heard Max's voice call out behind her she didn't stop.

'Ah, the working girl! Hard night's work?' he yelled scornfully.

She bit her lip and tried not to let herself get upset. This wasn't the moment to talk to him; she was too tired and all she wanted was to sleep. It was no use feeling sorry for herself; the whole ugly nightmare would be over soon.

In the morning, she prepared herself carefully so that he would have no complaints about her appearance. She found that it was difficult to eat breakfast because her nerves made her stomach flip every time she thought of Max watching her guiding the tours.

He hadn't appeared for breakfast, nor was there time to speak to him before she was obliged to begin conducting the first tour around. Disappointed, she threw herself into her job, only pausing for a brief, heart-flipping moment when she saw Max's noble head at the back of the group.

Considering her exhaustion, she managed well, though once or twice an exasperated note edged into her voice before she could help it. One or two visitors had no idea how to control their children! And it was awful, having Max looming directly in her line of vision, fixing her with his cold, judging eyes, waiting for her to make a mistake!

Three long, wearying days passed. Despite her asking for an appointment to see him, he kept out of her way so skilfully that their only contact was with their eyes, above the heads of visitors. It seemed he had no complaints.

She had called home and found that everyone was settling to the stand-in's methods, even if they did compare her unfavourably to Lucy. You couldn't expect the poor woman to understand that winding wool and sharing a magazine was an important part of life, and that time simply had to be found for looking relaxed and sitting with the residents.

Lionel was falsely cheerful, saying she wasn't missed apart from the chocolate cakes, and to enjoy her holiday, and that made her feel worse. Each time she felt more and more homesick.

And each time she hoped Selina would be at home, or that she would ring. And the relentless pace of work was beginning to tell. She'd overslept that morning and Max had told her she had to go into Stresa after work and buy a fork and trowel and then weed around the rows of palm trees after work. He was so cold and angry that Lucy knew instinctively it was a bad moment to ask for an appointment with him—and she didn't know when she could fit it in, anyway!

She'd skipped dinner and eventually found a hardware shop, but now she'd returned and only had half an hour before she had to be serving meals at the café! Lucy's face crumpled in sheer despair and helplessness as she saw the long row of palms in front of her.

'Earning a bit of pocket money?' came Jed's cheery tones. 'Hey, honey, don't get upset. What's happened?'

'I've got to weed these beds,' she said miserably. 'Max made me, because I was late.'

'Good lord! That's extraordinary! None of us get that treatment, only a severe verbal stripping. He does seem to have a different rule for pretty girls. I remember Selina getting the same orders.'

'I'm not pretty——'

'Sure you are, honey,' laughed Jed, putting his arm around her shoulders. 'Don't do it. He won't know.'

'I bet he intends to inspect the beds personally,' she sighed. 'I'll give them a quick turn with the trowel and hope he thinks I've done them properly.'

'I'll help you,' offered Jed, taking the fork from her tired, listless fingers.

Too grateful to protest, she smiled at him weakly and began to work.

They'd finished three beds, with three to go, crouching together in companionable silence, when Lucy became aware of a pair of charcoal-grey trousers and two belligerently shiny black shoes in front of her nose.

From her cramped, low position, Max Mazzardi looked even more intimidating than usual. His gaze swung to Jed, still in blissful ignorance and whistling as he weeded.

'Jed, I admire your interest in my garden, but I would be glad if you'd leave it alone,' said Max silkily.

'Oh! Well, I was just——'

'Yes, so I saw,' Max interrupted pleasantly. 'I want to talk to Lucinda alone. If you wouldn't mind?'

Jed stood up uncertainly. 'Max, this isn't like you. I don't know why you treat Lucy like this——'

'No, you don't,' grated Max. 'I hope you know me well enough to realise that there is a good reason and will allow me to speak to her in private.'

For a moment, Jed's eyes darted between Max and the wooden Lucy, and then he shrugged, leaving without a word.

She checked her watch and continued to weed frantically. Three more beds to do, and it was seven-twenty already!

'Don't involve Jed or anyone else in your extra duties again,' said Max icily. 'Or I'll make your life hell!'

'What makes you think you haven't done that?' she asked wearily, moving on to the next bed.

'Has your sister tried to contact you?' he snapped.

'No, she hasn't!' Lucy dug viciously at the deep-seated roots of a stubborn weed, wishing it was Max's impossibly shiny shoe.

'What are you doing after this?' he demanded.

'I'm washing the dirt off my hands and then I'm going out,' she said tightly.

'Stay,' he muttered. 'Let's talk. There's something going on I don't understand. You're full of contradictions. You are demure and neat at work, pleasant and patient and you have a flair for handling people—apart from one or two lapses. Yet sometimes you dress and move like a vamp. You turn up for work as if you've been dancing and making love all night, and yet you don't have the glow of a woman who is satisfied sensually. Lucinda...'

'I'm going out,' she said crossly, wondering if he intended to have her followed. 'I'll turn up on time and I'll do your wretched jobs. I made a couple of mistakes, but so does everyone when they're doing the tours. If it helps you to enjoy the knowledge, I'll confirm that you have, indeed made my life a hell. I'm very unhappy and I have discovered that I can hate someone so much that I feel like stabbing this fork through his foot and skewering him to the ground! So if I were you, I'd move away and let me get on!'

She bent her head, her vision blurred. There was the sound of soft footfalls, walking away. She rubbed her eyes dry, finished the weeding and steeled herself to face the next few hours.

She was very jumpy that evening at the *trattoria*, particularly when two policemen sauntered in, eyeing her with interest and sitting down at one of the tables she was in charge of.

Mustering a blank expression, she walked over quickly and handed them a menu, backing away so fast that she bumped into a man behind her. When his hands touched her shoulders she knew without turning who it was: no one else had such an instant, dramatic effect on her pulse-rate! Now he'd want to know what she was doing!

'Chatting up the local police? Hoping to keep them bribed?' he asked silkily.

'Excuse me, I have customers,' she said over her shoulder, feeling the hiss of his warm breath as it was suddenly exhaled. Slowly he turned her around, examining the white apron and her order-book that she was clutching.

In surprise he released her, and watched as she hurried to the kitchen on shaky legs. Lucy sighed. She couldn't stay in there all night. Head held high, she checked the other tables in case they needed clearing, and summoned up the courage to approach Max and the policemen. He was probably discussing ways to trace Selina, she thought.

'We'll have two veal, one chicken, a bottle of house white and mineral water.'

'Carbonated?' she asked coolly.

'Still,' he answered wryly. 'When do you finish?'

'When the washing-up has been done,' she snapped, whirling away.

Every time she came to the table, she felt his eyes on her, dark and unfathomable. It was an odd sensation, serving him, and she decided she didn't like it one bit. In fact, any situation where she was subservient to him she disliked intensely.

The men stayed a long time, talking, drinking coffee and brandies, then finally paid the bill and left without leaving any tip. She stacked the plates, all of her customers now gone. Steadily she tackled the dishes, finding them a good solid reminder of her position in life.

The owner paid her, smiled, said she was a good girl and patted her on the head affectionately. Max emerged from the shadows beneath a plane tree.

'This way.'

Too tired to argue, she followed him obediently, and when his hand clasped hers to help her on board his launch she felt her heart lurch crazily.

She sank back into the cushions, silence between them as he headed towards his island and then the engine cut out. The boat drifted gently on the black satin water.

'I'm listening,' he said quietly.

'Yes.' She was tired of shielding Selina, tired of working non-stop, tired of worrying about everyone at home. For once in her life she'd be selfish and do something for herself. Clearing her name in his eyes was the most important thing to her at that moment.

'Good. Let's start at the beginning. You've been working at the *trattoria* ever since you arrived?' he asked, sitting beside her.

'Yes.'

'That's why you were so late each night?'

She nodded and he gave an exclamation of impatience.

'Why on earth didn't you say?' he demanded.

'I didn't have much chance,' she answered wearily. 'You'd made your mind up what I'd been doing.'

'I was...' His dark brows knit together angrily. 'That first night, you were very dishevelled and it looked as though you were drunk, too. You passed out, after all.'

'No. Not drunk, just very, very tired.'

'Hell! You stupid... Why have you taken the job?' he asked shrewdly.

'I have no money. I had to pay the hotel bill somehow.'

'Surely you came prepared? You must have brought enough with you!'

'I did. Selina... Oh, Max, she was so frightened! She had to do it. She took my money while I was having dinner with you. Every last penny. And all my clothes.

Everything,' she said dully, miserable at betraying her sister.

'Oh, dear heaven!' he breathed, taking her in his arms. 'What an awful experience!'

Lucy clung to him, her face against his chest and feeling an inexpressible relief that he believed her. Something soared within, like a bird suddenly released and able to fly again.

'You idiot,' he said gently, stroking her hair. 'If only you'd said... Hell, I must have been an ogre to stop you confiding in me!'

'You were,' she whispered, content now.

'I'm sorry,' he muttered against her ear. 'You must be so desperately exhausted.' His mouth nuzzled the lobe and the change from kindly apology and sympathy to slow sensuality alerted every alarm in Lucy's body.

'Don't do that!' she cried, pushing him away and retreating to a far corner of the boat. She didn't trust herself to keep resisting him. His insatiable virility was not going to be assuaged by her!

'Lucinda...'

'Please, Max. You have to accept that I'm not your kind of girl——'

'Oh, you are, very much so,' he crooned.

Her body strained towards him and she impatiently tensed, forcing herself to reject him.

'No, I can't get involved with you,' she said coldly. 'I don't want to.'

'Your body does,' he murmured, reaching out a finger and running it down her bare arm.

She was unable to prevent her head from going back and a moan escaping from her parted lips, or stop the quiver that his touch evoked.

'That's because you're very experienced and know how to seduce women,' she said in a low tone. 'And because I'm inexperienced and not used to bold men.'

'I thought so.' He smiled.

'That still doesn't give you the right to flirt,' she said shakily. 'Soon, when all this is sorted out, I'll be going home. What's the point in doing something we'll both regret?'

'I think you're tired,' he said indulgently. 'Let's get you back. I knew I was right about you. You can stay at the palazzo and wait for Selina. In the morning, I'll send Paolo to settle your bill and tell the *trattoria* owner that you won't be coming in again.'

'I couldn't ask you to pay for me!' she protested.

'And I can't stand by and see you sacrifice yourself for others,' he growled. 'It seems to me that you're far too loyal. That sister of yours doesn't deserve you. When the police find her she'll get a nasty shock. Tonight I was told that she'd get at least ten years for fraud and deception.'

'Max!' she gasped in horror. 'You can't send her to gaol! It's not her fault what happened. I know who took the money and the jewels, it was your brother Renzo, he——'

'*Basta!*' he snapped, and then continued more gently, but still with a steely note in his voice, 'You mustn't repeat gossip. We will discuss further in the morning. But I will not have you making accusations against my brother. Do you understand?'

'Max,' she said brokenly, 'I'd do anything to stop you gaoling Selina. She's innocent!'

'I don't want to hurt you,' he said quietly. 'But I can't protect you from the consequences of other people's actions. Justice must be done. Selina has behaved like a tramp...'

'You have no proof of that! You're judging her by the way she looks and...'

'Lucinda, see your half-sister clearly for once! She tried to blackmail us all,' he said, watching her reaction.

'Blackmail?' she breathed.

'Yes. She made damn sure that I'd find her in bed with Renzo by calling me to his room.'

'No!' she cried, refusing to believe that Selina could go so far for the man she loved. Then she remembered her story about trying to seduce him. Surely... her huge eyes scanned Max's face, seeing pity there.

'Renzo was asleep,' he said sternly. 'She'd crept in beside him to cause trouble—and perhaps to persuade him to make love to her, since I gather he'd refused to dishonour her before marriage. Selina was lying there as bold as brass, and when I came in she said I'd have to let them marry or she'd tell everyone she'd been seduced. The police want me to add blackmail to the indictment. That will increase her sentence even more.'

Lucy struggled to keep her head clear and not let the terrible revelations swamp her. 'Selina is misguided...'

'She is a menace,' he grated. 'And ought to be put away.'

'Please, ask what you want of me, let the police find her and bring her here, but please, please, withdraw the charges!' Tears began to well in her eyes and she angrily dashed them away. 'Think of my stepfather. The news of Selina's imprisonment and disgrace would kill him! He dotes on her!'

'Too much, it seems,' said Max grimly.

'You must relent,' she persisted, clutching his arms and gazing at him as if her own life depended on his capitulation. 'You can't be so cruel, so heartless.' In the back of her mind, she remembered everything she'd been told about this man: that once crossed he was implacable in his revenge. 'Anything!' she cried with desperate recklessness. 'I'll do anything!'

'I want to make love to you,' he muttered throatily.

'Oh, lord!' Her hands fell away and she stared at him helplessly.

The look in his eyes made her body flow. Imperceptibly, his tongue slicked over his lips and her fascinated gaze followed its movement, a wild churning erupting inside her. She felt the gentle lethargy creep over her and this time it was nothing to do with being tired, but a slow and pleasurable arousal.

Max made no movement towards her, but she was aware that he had tensed every muscle. A heat emanated from him, and with it an intangible force which was drawing her to him and towards shame.

'I want you so much that I can think of nothing else,' he breathed. 'I want to possess you before any other man. To teach you about lovemaking before anyone else spoils it for you. I want to take your head in my hands and learn every expression that flits across your face, to know the places in your body which thrill to my touch, to show you the ultimate pleasure our bodies can create. And I want to begin the journey of knowing you now, Lucinda.'

Her head spun. His eyes were so mesmeric, so deeply probing her soul, his body so incredibly desirable to her, that she knew it was only a matter of time before he reached out and began that journey. She hated herself for wanting him so desperately; reviled her body for even contemplating the act of love with a man she had no intentions of marrying.

'I'm tired,' she whispered, her eyes huge as her reluctant words were forced out. 'I'm not thinking clearly.'

'I'm not sure I want you to,' he said drily.

'Can we go back now?' she asked in a small voice.

'Does that mean "no"?'

'It means I'm very tired,' she moaned.

'Stalling for time again?' he asked bitterly.

'Please!'

Without a word, he stood and moved slowly over to the wheel, starting the engine and taking them back to the island, his back and leg muscles rock hard.

'I'd rather you found your own way up to your room,' he said huskily. 'I can't be sure that I wouldn't follow you in.'

Lucy couldn't look at him. Instead she forced herself to move as naturally as possible, and only when she was in her room did her shaking legs give way so that she staggered on to the bed and fell asleep immediately, fully dressed.

The next morning, thankful that Max wasn't around at breakfast time, she turned her mind to working hard, and as she gained confidence she began to enjoy herself, especially now that she knew that she wasn't working at the *trattoria* and could relax that evening. She'd somehow talk Max around about Selina. Perhaps she could even persuade his grandmother to intervene. When she finished the last session, Paolo brought a message from Max. Dinner at seven-fifteen, drinks at seven in the salon.

Her opportunity. Providing she kept cool and self-contained, and didn't let his good looks and tormented soul get to her heart, she'd be all right!

'Evening, Max,' she said brightly, inwardly groaning. He was wearing a charcoal-grey silk dinner-jacket, with a fine black stripe and black satin lapels, with a black satin bow tie. He looked devastating, his dark eyes hooded and wary, the pure, chiselled lines of his face under tight control.

'Good evening. What can I get you to drink?' he asked smoothly.

'White wine?' she suggested.

He handed her the cold glass and motioned her to a chair. There was a gentle swish of silk as he sat, and she found that she was trembling, trying not to look at him. Everything depended on the way she conducted herself, and she didn't want to spoil her sister's future by letting her own desire blind her to practicalities.

'Grandmamma will be coming soon,' he murmured, sending her into a panic. She hadn't wanted to hurry her speech!

'Max——' She paused, trying to pluck up courage.

'Yes?'

Lucy had the impression he didn't intend to make things easy for her. His voice was slightly mocking.

She raised solemn eyes to him. 'I ask you to give Selina and Renzo a chance. Wait until they return before you carry out your threat to contact the police. They'll bring the money back, I'm sure.'

She prayed that Renzo could be persuaded to do so. He couldn't be all bad.

'Why should I be so generous?' asked Max, his lips glistening with wine. He leaned back in the chair, completely at ease, and rested one soft, leather-clad foot on his knee. The deceptively casual gesture only served to emphasise the strength in his thighs.

Lucy tore her gaze away and stared at her glass, taking a long sip. 'You would avoid public scandal,' she suggested quietly.

'And you think I care about the Mazzardi family?' His eyebrow rose sardonically.

'Yes, I do,' she said. 'I think you care very much, but you wouldn't dream of letting anyone know that. I think you cared for your father, too, but are reluctant to say so in case it makes you vulnerable.'

'Well, well,' he drawled, rising with a swift movement and refilling his glass. Hers had also been topped up before she could stop him. 'You have been doing a lot of thinking. However,' he continued, standing in front of her, swilling the wine around gently before tossing it down, 'you forget one thing. My pride. I can't be seen to be weak. So I must act harshly where your thieving sister is concerned, whatever my inner feelings.'

Lucy stared at his impassive face. She had met her match. He was a man who held his hurt inside, whose volcano of emotion was ruthlessly suppressed, who stood apart from society and manipulated it to suit him. To him, obstacles were for stepping over in the relentless journey to his goal.

'There is one thing that would make me change my mind,' he said softly.

She heard the persuasive, sensual hunger in his words, and a bolt of pure electric response shot through her body. The distance between them seemed bridgeable, their flesh joined by sexual tension.

Lucy's mind snapped out with an answer to defuse his overwhelming magnetism.

'A brain transplant?' she suggested.

He dazzled her with a grin, and she sank deeper into his snare with the transformation of his features.

'You are very resilient. I do believe you could master anything you wanted to,' he murmured.

'Or anyone,' she countered with confidence.

'Not quite. You see, as far as I am concerned, you are in my debt and owe me a great deal.'

'You'll be repaid,' she said quickly.

'I know I will.' The tone was suddenly menacing. 'Because I have decided that my price for silence and for playing the waiting game is going to be paid as I suggested earlier. I promise your sister will not go to prison. In exchange...' His eyes kindled. 'I want you.'

'So you said.' Lucy clenched her teeth together. He hadn't persisted before. With any luck, his grandmother would come in and she'd be released from his intolerable gaze.

'But this time I mean it. Take it or leave it.'

Lucy gasped at his cold approach. 'You can't make arrangements with people like that!' she cried. 'Sex isn't like ordering a meal!'

'As you wish,' he shrugged. 'I hope your stepfather is well enough to stand the journey to Milan gaol when he visits Selina.'

'You swine!' she breathed, her face white.

'It's your choice,' he reminded her, with a bitter mouth. 'Not many women would refuse my offer. I am not an inexperienced lover.'

'That doesn't surprise me in the least!' she snapped. 'With that kind of approach, I should think you have plenty of practice in bedding new women. You'd never keep any relationship going for long.'

'Not so,' he said huskily. 'I have only been involved in long-term relationships with women...'

'I don't want to hear!' said Lucy quickly. She was distressed to know that other women had clung to him, shared his bed, touched with their fingers that curving mouth. Oh, drat him!

'Lucinda,' he whispered, putting aside his glass and removing hers from nerveless fingers. He knelt in front of her and caressed her knee. She gave a sharp intake of breath and his fingers paused, then continued to send rivers of delight to her loins. His face was bent; all she could see was his thick fringe of black lashes sweeping the high cheekbones and his black glossy hair, touchable, smelling faintly of shampoo.

'Lucinda,' he said again, his voice deep with passion, 'I can't seem to break down your reserve. I can't touch you mentally. But I can reach you physically, I know that. I want you so much that I'm prepared to use any means to get you into my arms.' His hand slid up her thigh, pushing away her skirt, and she gripped his wrist in fear. The dark wells of his eyes compelled her. Calmly, deliberately, he reached up and cupped her breast, his lashes flickering at her involuntary shiver of pleasure. He watched her face, seeing the weakness there, the flushed bloom on her skin and the sensuality which told him that his seduction was effective.

'One night in your arms,' he murmured. 'If I can have nothing else, give me one night.'

CHAPTER NINE

'Max,' she whispered hoarsely, her eyes luminous, 'I love my sister and I'd do almost anything for her. But I also respect myself. Neither Selina nor I would casually give ourselves to a man. We've been brought up to value our own bodies. I want to give my virginity to my future husband and so does she.'

His hand was motionless as he searched her face. Then he rose, and as he did so the Contessa entered the room. Max half turned to Lucy, a cynical smile about his mouth.

'Incredible timing,' he said shakily. 'Don't you think?'

Weak from emotion, aware of how deeply she had affected him, Lucy admired his self-control, whatever she thought of his morals. Throughout the meal, she was to admire him more. His grandmother, dressed more elegantly tonight in black crêpe and with her hair coiled up and adorned with feathers, was acidic in her remarks towards Max.

Lucy felt chewed up inside, and several times her eyes strayed to him, trying to offer silent sympathy, but he steadily ignored her and concentrated on his plate, drinking too much, too often.

The delightful little room, elaborately painted in classic style and furnished with period furniture, was an inappropriate setting for a character assassination.

They had reached the cheese course when Max's grandmother dropped her bombshell.

'It'll be so lovely to see Renzo again,' she sighed. 'We'll have parties once more. Massimo never gives parties. Never takes me shopping.'

'There's a possibility that Renzo may not come back,' said Max, stony-faced.

'Of course he is! He said so in his letter. Now, where is it...' She began to rummage in her handbag, and Lucy and Max stared at each other in stunned shock.

'Renzo has written to you?' grated Max.

'Well, he certainly wouldn't write to you; after all you did to break up his engagement,' said the Contessa sharply.

'I would like to read the letter.'

Not by a tremor in his voice did Max betray what he must be thinking and feeling. He accepted it graciously from his grandmother.

'Read it out,' she said imperiously. 'I'd like to hear it again.'

Max's chest rose and fell briefly, and he began to read in a monotone.

'Darling Grandmamma, I beg your forgiveness for leaving without saying goodbye. I know you'll understand when I say it was the only thing to do because I couldn't fight Massimo, he's too strong for me.'

'Poor boy,' muttered the Contessa.

Max glared and continued. 'We are now...' Max's lips drew into a thin line. '...married by special dispensation. We are coming home for your blessing, and hopefully Massimo's. Tell him, and ask Lucy to forgive us too for taking her things. It was my idea. We knew she'd be all right because she's so obviously honest that Massimo would see she didn't suffer.' He put the letter down and stared at Lucy with an ironic twist to his mouth.

'Does he say anything about the money from the safe, or the jewels?' asked Lucy quietly. The news of her sister's marriage should have been thrilling. All she could think of, however, was the threat hanging over Selina's head and what Max would do, now that his offer of a one-night stand had been rejected—and the reason had been made redundant.

'Nothing.' Thoughtfully he returned the letter.

'Will you accept their marriage?' pleaded his grandmother. 'You are the head of the family. Your approval is important.'

The silence grew. 'I accept, but I don't approve,' said Max finally.

'Why?' Lucy asked.

'I have yet to be convinced that Selina is honest and in love,' he said darkly.

'How would you ever recognise love? You have no heart!' snapped the Contessa. 'I welcome the marriage. At least Renzo is on the way to fulfilling his duties by producing heirs, which is more than you've done!'

'The men in this family have always married for love. Would you want me to settle for less?' he asked quietly.

A particle of ice seemed to enter Lucy's heart. He seemed very alone.

'You'll never find a wife by working all hours that God gave you,' said his grandmother sternly. 'Be like Renzo, go to parties, give parties...'

'I'm too busy at the moment, making sure this place doesn't fall apart,' he seethed, on the edge of his patience. 'Is that what you really want? For me to throw parties so soon after my father's death?'

'Why not? You never loved him!'

Max met Lucy's eyes and rose to their challenge. 'I did, Grandmamma. I loved him dearly, as I love you all.'

'You've never shown it,' said his grandmother uncertainly. 'We could never cuddle you, like Renzo.'

'Oh, why do you keep pushing Renzo down Max's throat?' cried Lucy in despair. 'Can't you see how hurtful it is?'

'Renzo needs reassurance! Massimo never needed anyone to tell him he was capable,' said the Contessa. 'It was all too apparent. He was so superior in everything he did that we had to take him down a peg or two occasionally. He was better than Renzo at everything. He outswam everyone in Stresa, was taller, stronger, more self-assured. He was always captain of the school team, popular at school and highly talented. It was his poor brother who had the inferiority complex. We had to boost his morale all the time. With an intimidating brother like Massimo, it's hard to see any good in yourself.'

'I don't believe it!' muttered Lucy.

'What?' rapped the Contessa.

'None of that success matters,' said Lucy gently. 'It's the warm regard of the family that is important. It's important to Max, I know.' She glanced anxiously at him and her heart appeared to tumble to a shuddering stop before picking up its beat again, for there was a smile on his face so broad that it was as if he'd unlocked his very soul and was delighted with what he had found.

'He needs your love and support. He's sacrificed a great deal,' she said breathlessly, taking advantage of the old lady's astonished silence. 'He has great responsibilities—more than any of us.'

'Not you. You have a whole houseful of old crones like me to care for,' she said, her sharp eyes on Lucy.

'Max has a business and employees who rely on him to make the right decisions. He's worried sick about it, and...'

'You never told me that!' Max's grandmother rounded on him.

'What was the point? You never showed any interest in my life in England. You resented the fact that I was there, and changed the subject every time I began to tell you what I'd been doing.'

'I—I'm sorry,' said his grandmother.

At the sight of the old lady's moist eyes, Max rose quickly, dropping his linen napkin on the table, and putting his arms around her while she sobbed and muttered into his chest. Lucy left quietly, happy that there were signs of a reconciliation between Max and the Contessa.

Maybe the mellow Max would be kind to Selina and Renzo. She wished she knew how long it would be before they returned. Could she stay? Dared she stay, with Max so obviously hungry for her? Lucy sighed. He needed her in the same way the old people at home needed her: as a gentle mother-figure. For once in her life, she would like to be desired as a woman!

'Wait!' came Max's command.

'No,' she said, turning on the stairs. 'Your grandmother needs you.'

He ran up lightly. 'She's all right. I came to tell you that your room has been changed. I'd better come with you and show you where you are.'

There was nothing for it but to let him accompany her, though she didn't speak. Yet she was acutely aware of his physical presence, one step behind her, and of his regular breathing. She heard the movement of his soft silk suit and a waft of fresh aftershave drifted over her shoulder. His hand splayed out on the banister, just below hers, big, with long, sensitive fingers. Fingers that would be able to arouse her to secret, private delights, if she ever once encouraged him.

Selina had found her ideal lover; she had taken the step of marriage into this noble family. Lucy wanted Max, but knew the stakes were too high for him, for any man. And however much he thought he needed her, that need was no substitute for love, for a partnership of two equal people.

'To the right.'

He indicated the way, being careful not to touch her, and eventually she reached the private suite of rooms and was shown into a large bedroom with a canopied bed and a thick carpet, both in the same powder blue.

'Why move me here?' she asked.

'You're too good for the attic.' He smiled crookedly.

'Thank you,' she said, emotionally exhausted. She could sleep for days! 'Goodnight,' she said sharply.

He didn't take the hint. 'I have to thank you for defending me,' he said.

She walked to the dressing-table, absently undid her ribbon and ran her fingers through her hair. 'I couldn't stand it any longer,' she said. 'Your grandmother is actually very nice, but she had a block where you were concerned.'

'I'm almost glad that Selina hit our family with all the subtlety of a bulldozer.' He smiled wryly. 'Otherwise you would never have come out of hiding.' In a couple of quick strides he had crossed the room and had swept one arm around her waist, pulling her against him. His other hand caressed her shoulder.

Lucy's startled eyes flashed at him in the mirror. His body was warm and inviting. She was so small, so dainty in comparison with him, and his heart was beating a rapid tattoo against her shoulder-blade. He must respect her! She was his sister-in-law! 'No!' she croaked. 'Is this why you moved me from that attic? So that the bed and its surroundings would be more to your liking?'

He laughed, the beauty of his face making her ache with longing and despair.

'No, madonna. I merely wanted you to be more comfortable. That attic was too spartan for you.'

'Not for Selina, though! I'm the one who is used to hardship, and yet you made her live in it. If it's good enough for her, then it's good enough for me. I want no favours from you. Kindly arrange for my—Selina's things to be taken back,' she said proudly.

'Don't be ridiculous,' he said gently. He drew her into his arms and she struggled to be released.

'You can't use me! You can't keep me a prisoner and do what you like with me. I'm not your possession! Leave me alone!' she cried fiercely.

'I realise that. Stop fighting yourself. You have a passionate heart beneath that no-nonsense, common-sense exterior. Let's...' His fingers trailed down her arm. 'Let's explore it together.'

'No, thank you,' she said stiffly, gritting her teeth for defence. Please don't let me give in, she prayed.

'Don't you trust me?'

'I don't trust any men. I've been let down before.'

'Why was that? What was missing in their characters? Were they two-timers?' he asked gently.

She was tempted to say something snappy, but made the mistake of looking into his eyes and felt compelled to tell the truth.

'Lame dogs,' she muttered. They all were. She'd been used.

'It's not surprising,' he said heartlessly. 'You are far too unselfish, sweet and generous. I never knew that such women existed. Don't you really know what I feel for you?' he asked, his face becoming filled with lazy sensuality.

Lucy felt defenceless under the impact of his carnal, smouldering gaze. Despite herself, despite her deep sense of morality, she was being drawn irresistibly to him, as spirals of dizzy excitement whirled within her body, creating a storm of feeling.

'N-n-no,' she stammered, as his arms tightened like a steel band around her and she was crushed against his body even harder. The consuming heat of his desire burned shockingly into her, causing a spasm to pass throughout her body so that she trembled and quivered like a slender stem.

'It's about time you learnt,' he murmured, turning her around.

Mesmerised, her slowly-moving brain incapable of making her limbs work, Lucy watched as his mouth parted and his eyes grew even more slumbrous.

'No,' she croaked hoarsely. 'You mustn't!'

'Why?' he asked, his head already bending towards her, his eyes demanding her submission.

She was bent back slowly, her supple body still trembling as she resisted. 'Without love...' she whispered, her throat terribly dry.

His relentless mouth came nearer. 'I'm doing everything I can to remedy that problem,' he breathed.

'But...'

He had caught her off guard and his warm mouth fastened on hers, his eyes dark and turbulent in passion and determination.

She took a deep, panicky breath as he ravaged her neck with his scorching kisses.

'Max——'

'No,' he grated hoarsely, his searching, ruthless mouth moving to her shoulder. 'You've driven me crazy over the last few days. Heaven help me, I'm losing control!'

Her heart thudded like a hammer at the passion in his voice that held so much yearning and which so closely echoed her own desperate need for him that she almost relented. His silken jaw was sliding along her skin as he kissed her shoulder and teased its hollows with his tongue, and she found herself clutching blindly at him and her body dissolving.

She wanted to give herself to him, to hold nothing back, to lose herself in his arms. The misery of the situation overcame her and she began to sob loudly.

Max drew away slowly, shaking visibly. Then he pulled her head into his chest and stroked her head while she cried, his fingers threading through her mane of hair.

'What am I going to do with you?' he sighed.

'You—you could l-l-leave me alone!' she sniffed.

'That would be silly,' he reasoned.

'I want to go home,' she cried into his shirt.

'You will wait till your sister comes. And even then I intend to keep you here till we have settled things between us.'

She gripped his lapels tightly and stared up at him. 'So I am your prisoner again, then,' she said bitterly.

His long black lashes flickered on to his taut cheekbones, and then he looked her straight in the eyes.

'No,' he said solemnly, 'I am yours.'

Her eyes lashed him with contempt. 'Don't you *dare* to make fun of me!' she seethed.

'I would never make fun of you. With you,' he grinned, his eyebrows devilish, 'but never *of* you. Lucinda, you captured me the first time we met. It was like being hit by a steam-train. I've never recovered.'

'You were out for a good flirt,' she accused.

'I wasn't flirting, and you know it!' He frowned and his eyes devoured her. 'I looked at you and instantly knew why I'd been holding back on all the other women in my past. I saw within you a depth of loving, tenderness, caring, that I had despaired of ever finding. I was suddenly complete, Lucy. I saw a promise of the future and it looked good.'

'Oh, Max!' she breathed miserably.

'My angel,' he sighed, reaching for her arms and moving closer, 'I will not let you go. I refuse to accept the idea that this was destined to be a brief, painful meeting and a traumatic parting.'

His hands began to move gently over her flesh, and she placed her palms against his chest in protest.

'Don't do that!' she husked.

His mouth curved into a delightful smile, and as one hand slid to cradle the back of her head she gave a long, shuddering breath, the slow, heavy rhythm of the pulses in her body making her acutely aware of the sensation of deep lethargy. Then his mouth was pressing its velvet warmth into her neck, along the line of her shoulder, and with a brief, impatient exclamation he jerked her into his hard, unyielding, masculine body.

She gasped at the dangerous animal heat emanating from him, trembling from the feel of his hard, muscular thighs against her nakedness, the soft press of her breasts against his chest and the violent thudding of his heart.

His lashes flicked over her, down to the swelling, pearly globes, and his breathing rasped into her face.

'I can't let you go,' he muttered roughly. 'Not until I have you all, body and soul.'

Lucy's eyes grew huge at the threat as she fought to disregard the lethal caress of his hand in her hair and the urgency of her own body which was hurtling her towards the brink of control.

Max's mouth swooped down to hers, masterfully forcing open her lips with his insistent tongue. The sensation that followed, of warm, moist, erotic invasion, made her legs turn to water and she went limp in his arms. His muscles tensed to hold her, he swept her up and strode to the bed.

'No, Max,' she whispered, as he stood hesitantly, staring down at her, the wild beating of his heart sending a frisson of fear through her body.

'I want you, Lucinda,' he whispered, kissing her parted lips. 'And I love you, very much. I never believed I would ever say that. I love you. Love you.'

His words startled her, made her head spin. He only imagined that. He couldn't... Almost beyond sanity, the kiss became hard and he ravaged her with his mouth, his fingers gripping her delicate flesh and bone with such ferocity that she feared for her virginity. She recognised how close he was to unleashing his intemperate sexuality on her, how determined he was to take her and brook no refusal.

Frantically she beat on his hard chest, making little impact, the weight of his mouth and head so great that she couldn't twist from his brutal kisses.

'You won't deny me,' he urged, his voice thick with desire, the raw, naked hunger in his half-closed eyes making her body leap with longing. 'Somehow I have to show you my feelings. This is the only way I know, the only way I think you'll abandon all your rationalising and surrender to your emotions.'

'Put me down,' she whispered, with a sob. 'I can't bear this. I hate what you're doing to me. I'm not a cheap plaything, Max. Can't you see how much I dislike this?'

His mouth twisted. 'No, I can't. I can see that you want me. You are highly aroused. Only your head, your damn, stubborn head, refuses to admit that!'

'Put me down,' she said quietly, seeing that his feverish assault had been halted. She believed that he had enough honour not to hurt her, and to respect her wishes.

He swayed, a look of pain on his face. The dark, tanned face tilted back for a moment, and then he slid her abruptly to the ground and turned his back, its huge expanse held tense as he fought for control.

'You can't keep doing this to me! It's tearing me apart! You don't know how far you're pushing me, how great is my self-control. I know how I feel, Lucinda,' he groaned. 'I know how you feel. Where have I gone wrong?'

'By forgetting my responsibilities and our wildly differing backgrounds,' she whispered. 'There's no way we can have any kind of meaningful relationship hundreds of miles apart.'

'What do you mean?' he demanded, still refusing to look at her.

She heaved a great sigh. 'You have to live and work here and I have to live and work in England. Even if Renzo takes over here and you return to your office, I must put my family and the residents first, and you must put your work first.'

'There are difficulties. They can be surmounted.'

'Max, I don't have a job. I have a way of life. I'm on twenty-four-hour call. How can we get to know each other properly?'

'Work part-time. I'll pay for a relief.'

He was saying anything that came into his head to win her over. He couldn't see that he'd tire of her, once he'd found out how dull and uneventful her life was.

'No. I want to be free from personal relationships. Don't you understand?'

He spun on his heel. 'Lucinda,' he muttered brokenly, the anguish in his face tearing into her heart. 'I can't live without you.'

She forced herself to reject him. She hadn't said she loved him, had she? It was difficult to remember. But she must keep her head, ice him out.

'Don't use histrionics on me,' she said shakily.

'Damn you!' he roared, striding towards her.

'Max,' she cried, fending him off with her hands, 'for both our sakes, see sense! You're building this up into something bigger than it really is! Because I've refused you . . . am I the first woman to do so?'

'Yes, dammit, you are!' he whispered.

Lucy wasn't surprised. If she wasn't trying to protect herself from greater hurt, she would be in his arms and tearing at his shirt, encouraging him to love her with all the fury of his hot Italian blood.

'You can't win them all,' she said assertively.

'I don't want them all. I want you.'

'But only because you can't have me!' she said, exasperated.

'No. Because every minute I'm away from you there's an emptiness. Because I want to be with you every second of the day, because I've wasted years by not knowing you, and I can't lose any more of my life, our future.'

'We have no future,' she raged, beside herself with wanting him and knowing how futile that was. How could she ask him to live with her at Park View? He'd hate it. And she'd worry herself sick if she went to live with him. Stalemate.

'Lucinda!' Pain filled his eyes. 'Are you telling me that you don't need me? That you're going to walk out of here?'

'Yes! You're very attractive, Max, and would turn any girl's head.' She bit her lip at his harsh exhalation. 'But I must go home. There are ten people who need me.'

'Anyone can do your job! *I* need you!' he thundered.

'Not as much as them,' she defended, her chin held high. 'They need someone to look after them. They need my love!'

'Hell, I need that, too. I want your love!' he cried.

'Well,' she said, her heart thumping madly from nerves, 'you're not going to get it from me.'

A cold ice spread into the muscles of his face. 'You love ten elderly people, you want them, more than me? Is that the depth of your feelings for me?'

She swallowed to moisten her throat and make her voice ring clear and true. 'Correct.'

'We could work something out——'

'Why?' she asked lightly. 'Better to part as friends and call it a day.'

'You don't feel strongly enough to sit down and discuss the situation? To find a way around our obligations?'

'What for?' she asked quietly.

'I see.'

Lucy watched as he rocked on his heels, drawing in a huge breath and clenching his fists till the knuckles went white.

'I'm sorry. My own wishes made me blind to yours,' he breathed.

'They did,' she gulped.

'I want you out. Out of my life. Before I make a fool of myself again and beg for what I can never have. I'd be glad if you left in the morning. I have no wish to see you again. I'll arrange your flight for you. Allow me to lend you the money. I can get it from Selina when she appears,' he said in a toneless voice.

'Thank you.'

His eyes slowly travelled down her body, effectively stripping her in one long, last hungry look. Then he swung his panther shoulders around and strode quickly out of the room.

CHAPTER TEN

LUCY didn't cry: she dared not. If she showed herself the slightest sign of weakness, she would have given in to her own selfish needs and begged Max to make love to her.

Once he'd asked her to give him one night, and now, with lonely and passionless years ahead, she almost wished that she'd had the courage to throw away all her inhibitions and say yes. For Lucy knew that she wanted no other man but Max, would love no other man but him.

Sleep was impossible, of course. She had undressed and put on Selina's gorgeous nightie, but was still sitting on the bed where she'd staggered when Max had left. Now she must go over what happened so that she was certain she'd done the right thing in making her head rule her heart.

But her mind jumped about, from the way he had looked, to the bright face she must assume when she reached home, and then she thought of Selina. It would have been wonderful to see her—and hear her explanations! Restlessly Lucy jumped up and wandered about the room, then on impulse flung open the shutters to drink in the night air of Lake Maggiore for the last, sweetly painful time.

A light by the boathouse attracted her attention. There seemed to be two people coming up the path. Lucy's heart thudded. One was Selina! Hardly recognisable, in a dowdy dress, but it happened to be Lucy's smoky-blue one!

'Selina!' she yelled in delight.

Her sister looked up, scanning the dozens of windows, and then saw Lucy and waved. The dark, wavy-haired young man beside her grinned, his white teeth flashing in the darkness, and Lucy knew this was Renzo. They both looked so happy, hand in hand, smiling their intimate smiles, as they walked up through the terraces, and Lucy heaved a sigh of relief. One thing was all right, at least!

She motioned that she would be coming down and stepped out of the satin nightdress. Hastily the silky, lacy underwear was dragged on and then Selina's navy dress which seemed to do so much for her curves. In a flash, Lucy had hurtled out of the room and was running down the stairs and into Selina's arms.

'Lulu, Lulu, darling!' laughed Selina, quite breathless. 'Whatever is the matter? What are you saying?'

Lucy's hotly flowing tears prevented her from answering. All she could do was sob in great heaving breaths into Selina's shoulder. With loving arms around her, Lucy had given in to her misery, and it was a long time before she became coherent enough for Selina to push her away and help to wipe her eyes.

'I've never seen you cry. Renzo, I've never seen her cry!' said Selina in astonishment. 'Don't mope, darling Lucy, it's not like you. Aren't you keen to meet my heavenly husband?'

Lucy looked over the handkerchief and into Renzo's friendly brown eyes. 'Hello,' she said, with a brave smile.

'Hello, Lucinda,' he said kissing her on both cheeks. Then he looked from one to the other and began to laugh, shaking his head in amusement.

'And what's so funny?' frowned Selina.

'You two,' chuckled Renzo. 'You told me Lucy didn't bother to make the best of herself, that she wore frumpy clothes. Here she is, in a very sexy dress that clings to every inch, and with a mass of hair any man would long to get his hands into, and there you are, my sweet, in a faded, prim, shapeless outfit, with no make-up on and all the curl out of your hair. Funny, yes?'

The two sisters looked at each other and began to smile, then laugh, clutching each other wildly, both realising that the roles had more than changed outwardly: that Lucy had needed Selina and had been comforted.

'It's wonderful to see three people so happy,' came Max's icy tones.

Lucy sprang away from Selina, her heart thumping helplessly, her face still moist from tears. Max looked terrible, his eyes haunted and remote, his suit rumpled as if he'd been sleeping fitfully in it.

'Well,' said Max, looking around at the silent threesome, 'I seem to have stopped your fun. I assume, Renzo, you are intending to apologise to me for the trouble you've caused and will tell me what you are going to do about the missing money? We'd better go into the study.' He turned to Lucy. 'There's no reason for you to hang around. Go to bed.'

'You bully! Leave my sister alone!' cried Selina, enraged by Lucy's stricken face. 'She comes with us. We owe her an apology, too.'

'More than you know,' said Max grimly, striding ahead.

'Has he been a pig?' asked Selina in a hoarse whisper as they followed, she and Renzo supporting the trembling Lucy.

'Yes and no,' she said listlessly.

'That's no answer!'

Lucy shrugged. It was all she could manage to say at the moment. Her eyes had flicked up and seen Max was tearing at his tie and loosening his top shirt button. The beautiful golden satin of his throat made her want to moan. Instead she dropped her lashes and stared at her feet.

Max took up a position in front of the marble fireplace—the position of authority and dominance. He brooded at them all.

'From the beginning,' he said, softly, huskily. 'I want to know everything, from the time that money first disappeared. Who was it? You, Renzo? You, Selina?'

'Me,' said Renzo quickly. 'Long before Father died. I was bored, doing nothing. He wouldn't let me do anything at all. What else was there for me to do but spend money? I was to blame. I know you would have had it out with Father, but I didn't have your courage. I never have. Father admired you for that.'

'Don't invent things. He never admired anything I did.'

'What?' Renzo gaped in astonishment. 'He couldn't believe he'd fathered you, you were so brilliant at everything you did. So self-sufficient, so wary, so unwilling to compromise. He was incredibly jealous—as we all were.'

Lucy listened in silence. It was as she thought. People weren't awfully good at being generous with praise.

'That's why I felt an affinity for Selina,' said Renzo unexpectedly.

Lucy's head swivelled around in surprise.

'Don't take this as a personal criticism, Lucy; it isn't your fault, any more than our misunderstandings were Massimo's fault. I know that now. But you are like him.'

'I'm not a bit like him!' she said vehemently, her hair tossing in all directions.

'Yes, you are,' said Selina gently. 'You were always so capable. Whatever needed doing, you did it. You coped with the cooking, the housekeeping, the accounts, the shopping, you had time to be affectionate... What role was there for me to play, but the dumb blonde? It's no one's fault, and you did see me for what I was, but I had to go away to see that I didn't have to put on an act any more, that someone could love me for what I was, even if I'm not as good as you at all the things a woman can do well.'

Lucy just gaped. 'I'm... I'm not perfect, or capable. Things needed doing and I did them.'

Max had begun to prowl around the room in an irritated manner. 'Get on with the story,' he said to Renzo.

'Well, I got into debt and borrowed from the safe to pay off my debtors. I had to alter a couple of figures to do that,' he said shamefacedly. 'I regret what I've done, and if you wish to make charges then Selina will wait for me till I'm out of gaol. I'm prepared to serve my sentence.'

Max's piercing gaze speared Selina, who looked back steadily. 'He's penniless,' he said remorselessly. 'Homeless.'

'You devil!' breathed Lucy.

'It's all right,' said Selina quietly. 'That doesn't matter. We've found out what it's like to be hard up with no luxuries, and that we enjoy working hard together. We are determined to make a life for ourselves, whatever you decide. We're prepared for the worst, and it's brought us closer together.'

'Blind loyalty seems to run in your family,' said Max cynically.

'Both girls are gems,' said Renzo, drawing them to him.

'Yes,' said Max heavily. 'Go on.'

'Well, I was in a mess. Father died, Grandmother saw I was in a helpless state and sent for you. By then I was in love with Selina and you spat fire at me every time I tried to tell you about her. You'd already made up your mind, and, like Father, were too stubborn to budge.'

'I had only taken a boat ride with your boatman,' said Selina earnestly. 'It turned out to be a battle for my honour.'

Renzo saw Max's sardonically arching brow and broke in. 'I can assure you, I was the first man Selina had ever known,' he said in a low tone.

Max flicked a quick glance at Lucy and nodded. 'I apologise, then,' he said. 'I had good reason to believe my judgement was right, but I apologise because I was wrong.'

'You terrified Selina,' said Lucy furiously. 'You made her life a misery. Because of you, I had to leave home. I'd be there now, doing the ironing, instead of...' Her voice broke.

'Lucinda!' Max took a couple of steps forwards, anguish on his face, as if he intended to embrace her. And then he met her blazing eyes, the amber lights of warning matching the flame of her hair. His jaw muscles clenched.

'What is going on here?' demanded Selina. 'What's happened between you two? Don't say he's hurt you, Lulu! I know we shouldn't have taken advantage of you, but suddenly Max became fiercely opposed to our marriage and Renzo said it was the only way. I couldn't think clearly. We skipped off with your stuff because we were sure Max would look after you, with your air of innocence and sweet nature. He didn't treat you badly, did he?' she asked anxiously.

'No worse than he treats anyone else,' said Lucy dully.

'Well, that's not very nice,' muttered Selina.

'We didn't spend your money,' said Renzo hesitantly. 'Hand over her handbag, darling. Everything's there, Lucy. Forgive us?'

'Of course,' she said, seeing how sorry he was.

'Did Lucy know anything of your deceptions?' asked Max grimly.

'Nothing, of course she didn't! She was entirely innocent. You've only got to look at her to see the kind of girl she is,' said Selina.

The dark hooded eyes morosely toured Lucy's curving body. 'And the jewellery?' he murmured.

'What jewellery?' asked Renzo with a frown.

'Grandmamma's. She said it had been in the safe. Now the safe is empty, remember?' said Max in a dangerous tone.

'I don't know anything about that,' said Renzo with conviction. 'She used to keep it in the safe, and then took to stuffing it away in with Father's things in his dressing-room. You know how absent-minded she's getting. I expect it's around somewhere.'

Max swore and left the room.

'OK, sister,' said Selina. 'Now give. There's an odd atmosphere in this room and it's something to do with you and Max.'

'Nonsense. It's just that I did your job for a few days and our relationship was difficult because he was edgy.'

'Edgy? I'd say he'd gone overboard,' commented Renzo. 'Has he made a pass at you?'

'Max and Lucy?' asked Selina in surprise. Then she took a good long look at her sister and her trembling lips. 'Dear heaven!' she breathed. 'Is that right? Is that why you were so upset? Did he force himself on you?'

'No!' denied Lucy. 'He's not like that. He had the opportunity, but respected me.'

Selina began to pester Lucy for details, but she resisted. Renzo took Lucy's side, and she suddenly felt so drained that she said she had to sleep. In the morning she would take the bus to Milan and get on the first available flight. Nothing Selina could say would dissuade her, and eventually they took a tearful farewell, with promises to visit the Home and show Renzo off to everyone. Until then, the marriage was to be a secret, though Lucy was to prepare the way by dropping hints.

Lucy met Max on the landing. She made to brush past him but his hand detained her.

'Let me go,' she said numbly.

'Grandmamma's jewels are safe. She'd wrapped them up in one of Father's jumpers,' he said expressionlessly.

'Oh, good.'

'You don't want to yell at me for accusing your sister? For causing you such agonies?'

'I want to go home.'

'So do I,' he muttered.

'This is your home.'

'No. England is. Lucy, we must try to stay together.'

'Max, I'm very tired. I must get some sleep. Take care of Selina. She'll be a tremendous asset, you know.'

'She'll have to be,' he said wearily. 'I don't intend to stay.'

'Because of Renzo?' she asked scornfully.

'Yes, but not in the way you mean. So that he can make his own way without me breathing down his back. In the same way that Selina can make her mark without you being Miss Perfect all over the place.'

'I never knew!' she cried.

'Neither did I.'

Lucy gave a helpless lift of her shoulders and walked to her room. Too late, she discovered that Max was hard on her heels.

'We have to talk,' he said quietly.

'We've done that. Will you please leave me alone?'

'After you explain to me what the problems are. I want to know, for instance, why you'd been crying.'

'Relief at seeing Selina,' she said quickly.

He pushed her inside the bedroom and shut the door behind him. Lucy felt the fluttering of her heart, trapped within her ribcage. In the darkness, Max looked very threatening.

'I don't believe you,' he said.

'There couldn't possibly be any other reason,' she snapped, defying him with her huge eyes.

Max leaned against the door and folded his arms. 'When I first met you, I had a definite impression of someone who was pure and vulnerable, honest and caring. For a while, various things happened to disillusion me. But now,' he said, fixing her with a baleful look, 'I've returned to my original opinion of you.'

'Good,' she said, with a false brightness. 'I am pure, so you can forget any ideas you have by being in my room. I might be vulnerable, but I'm learning to take care of that problem. I'm honest and caring, and that's why I look after the people in the Rest Home.'

'Honest?' His eyes searched hers and then he had drawn her protestingly to him, refusing to take any notice of her struggles, his fingers closing around her arms in a grip of steel. She'd wanted him for so long that instantly she felt the flames of desire licking through her body as they touched, as he pressed her against his length, as she felt his hard, muscular frame and the faint drift of musky aftershave. 'If you are honest, then you'll answer me one question,' he said, more huskily than ever.

'No,' she croaked. 'Not one night, I've told you that before!'

He chuckled deep in his throat and one hand shifted to lazily tip up her chin so that she was forced to look at him. His eyes had grown hot and sensual, his mouth arching with desire, and Lucy feared for her honour. But he didn't kiss her as she expected. Instead, his fingers lightly touched her face, travelling over it so that every inch was sensitised to his touch.

'I would like to see that madonna smile once more,' he whispered.

'You will, when I leave this island!' She shook.

His relentless fingers slid to her ear and she tried to evade them, but his grip on her arm tightened. So she clenched her teeth and prepared to put up with the erotic sensuality of his touch as it caressed her neck and then her body. She held herself very stiffly, hoping he'd tire of her lack of response, every one of her muscles flexed in defence. But her body was treacherous. He could tell that her breasts were flowing with warmth, filling with fire. He could tell from her breathing that when he touched each nipple lightly on the outside of her dress it was all she could do not to encourage him.

And he could tell from her face, her honest, vulnerable face, that he was creating a bitter-sweet torment, a torture that she wanted to finish, and wanted to prolong.

'Now,' he whispered, 'I will repeat what I said earlier. I love you, Lucy. I want to marry you, and I believe that between us we can solve the problem of your responsibilities. So, what I wish to ask, and you must answer honestly, is . . . Do you love me?'

Lucy's eyes rounded and she blinked. Max wickedly, cruelly bent and kissed her, his mouth tender and persuasive, coaxing, teasing, gently touching, lifting and descending again.

A small moan escaped her. He smiled into her eyes and kissed her more deliberately. Then again, and again, and suddenly it was as if she was in a shower of kisses, every part of her face and neck, her shoulders, her hands, then his fingers were unbuttoning her dress and his mouth began to travel towards her painfully yearning breasts.

'Oh, Max!' she groaned.

'It's unfair,' he muttered, 'I know, but I'm like that.' He raised his head and kissed her sweetly on the mouth. 'Answer the question or I'll kiss you in places you didn't know existed,' he threatened.

'Max!'

He grinned a devilish grin and gently bit her chin. 'Or bite,' he said to himself. 'Here . . . and . . .'

'Max!' she cried in horror, trying to protect herself.

'Answer. Honestly.'

Lucy tried, she really tried, but the sensation of his mouth nibbling at her collarbone was too exquisite to bear. 'Please!' she moaned, shaking with desire. To her relief, the torment was temporarily halted. 'I—I——' She met his eyes and saw how anxious he was becoming, and realised that he had stopped breathing. She ought to lie; no one would blame her for making things easier for both of them. But she couldn't, not with his eyes so appealingly tender and uncertain. 'I love you, Max,' she said quietly. 'I wish I didn't, but I do.'

His hands fell away at her expression. 'I wonder why I'm not jumping for joy,' he muttered.

'Because you know as well as I do that we can't bring our lives together without sacrificing so much that we'll hate each other,' she said soberly.

'Go on,' he said, stalking over to a chair and sitting down.

Lucy needed to sit, too. Her legs wouldn't hold her up any longer. She perched on the bed, knowing that they could both talk openly now.

'Supposing we both return to England. You are trying to run your business, I am trying to run the Home. You drive down occasionally and take me out. You'll exert all your energy to seduce me because you are impatient and don't like waiting for anything.'

He smiled grimly. 'I've held back so far.'

'But now you know what I feel about you,' she pointed out.

'Are you saying I'm irresistible?' he enquired.

'I think that one night I might give way. And I'd regret that.'

'Why? I intend to marry you. If I had my way, I'd damn well marry you tomorrow!' he growled.

'Max, I told you, I'm on call at the Home all the time. Can you see yourself putting up with abandoning our plans for an evening out because one old lady wants me around? Or because Mother's arthritis is particularly bad? Do you want to be married to a woman who puts you second?'

He stared at her helplessly. 'All right,' he said, 'Now try this. We agree tonight never to see each other again... Ah, I think you felt that pain as badly as I did,' he said, watching her closely. 'Anyway, we go our separate ways. Imagine yourself at the Home. Imagine how you feel, as you go about your work. Miserable. Because you're denying something that's profound, Lucy. We don't just have a strong liking for each other, we don't just have a sexual attraction. It's everything. It's a totality of experience. You know that. We are complete together, incomplete apart. You'll be so unhappy that you'll spread unhappiness around you. What kind of life would that be for your parents?'

'But——'

'What would they say, if they knew? What would they advise you to do, your parents, and the other residents?'

'They'd tell me to be selfish. Max, you're not to tell them. I forbid you!'

'Sweetheart, I will make compromises, but you must show me first that you recognise that you have your own future, that your husband and children will be important to you,' he said gently.

'Children?' she whispered, her head whirling with images of dark-eyed children, serious and intent, with long black lashes... 'Oh, Max, you're too cruel!' she wailed.

'Well?' he pursued relentlessly.

'Yes,' she breathed. 'I want you, and I want your children. But how——'

'Simple,' he said, his voice a soft, throaty purr. 'I move my business. Lock, stock, and...er...barrel. We do not live in the Home, because you will have your own home to run. And soon there will be children.' His eyes gleamed at the slowly dawning madonna smile of hope on her face. 'We will find the best housemother in the country for the Home, and you—we—will spend a great deal of our time there. But I will come first most of the time. *Capisci?*'

'*Capisco,*' she said breathlessly, beaming at him.

'Come here and let me pin my love-token on you,' he murmured, bringing out the amber brooch. 'It is over four hundred years old. It was given to the first Signora Mazzardi and has been given in love ever since.'

In a daze, she glided over to him and his fingers shook so that it took him a long time to fix the brooch properly.

'Will your idea work? Will it really be all right?' she asked anxiously.

'It'll work because we want it to.' He smiled. 'I always get everything I want.'

'I think,' she said, glowing with joy, 'that applies to me, too.'

'Let's find out if I'm a handful in bed,' he grinned.

He stifled her protest with a tender kiss, and then she took his head in her hands and bestowed on him her madonna smile, and then, much later, gave the gift she had kept for the man who would become her husband.

Lucy and Max lay talking till dawn, planning their future, planning her birthday, though she'd had the most important present of her life. She told him about the scarf she was to receive from Mrs Baker, and he looked down on her in delight, and the love and tenderness within him was overwhelming.

Outside, as the sky turned pink and then golden, for a few magic moments the whole scene was suffused with amber light: the sky, mountains, hills and the lake. Then the light of day gave everything an intense clarity and the lake lay a silent witness to their love: deep, flowing, undying and timeless.

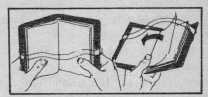